IF YOU NEVER COME BACK

SARAH SMITH

IF YOU NEVER COME BACK

For Stefanie. Thank you for believing in me.

PROLOGUE

Valentine's Day, this year

The second I set my eyes on Garret, I knew he would be good for one thing and one thing only: eye candy.

I was wrong. Sort of.

He is actually excellent eye candy. Six-foot-three, sandy blond hair, icy blue eyes, strong jawline. All of that on top of his build, which resembles that of an Olympic swimmer, and he's hands-down the best-looking guy in this bar.

But what's throwing me for a loop is his choice of conversation topic: eating pets.

"Kind of crazy, don't you think?" He gestures, martini in hand. "Weird that we think it's acceptable to eat cows and chickens, but not cats and dogs."

The frown on his face doesn't convey irony like I hope. Just pure, unfettered confusion. As if the single greatest mystery that exists on planet Earth is why we aren't all chowing down on our pets.

I drain my glass with a long sip, the vodka burning my tongue. I wince, longing for the taste of tequila instead.

I will the urge away. No tequila, not ever again.

Stacy the bartender offers a single sympathetic nod as she refills my glass, this time with top-shelf vodka. I open my mouth to request the cheaper vodka, but she answers with a pointed stare. *No need to explain,* she wordlessly says. *You have to listen to this guy talk about eating kittens and puppies on a date. The least I can do is offer a few splashes of decent alcohol.*

And this is how I spend Cupid's special day, sitting across from a hunky weirdo in the bar where I work part-time, trying not to choke on my drink.

Thank heavens that my cousin Remy isn't here. He owns this bar, the Dandy Lime, and if he overheard this guy, he would immediately call him out. Ask him at maximum volume why Garret's chatting about such a creepy topic. It would be entertaining and embarrassing. I love Remy to death, but it would cause a scene.

"Um, what now?"

I don't even bother to hide the disgust in my response. I cross my arms and lean back on my barstool, widening the space between us. Garret carries on, unbothered by my reaction. Evidently, he can't tell by my body language and dead silence over the last few minutes that I'm just not into this conversation.

He flashes a toothy grin, that same one that made my stomach flip when we locked eyes while perusing the stacks at the bookstore yesterday. That grin must be a decoy he uses to rope unsuspecting women into dates before he drops the bomb that he advocates for eating pets.

He rests his hand over my hand that's sitting on the bar top. His clammy palm feels like a giant slug on my skin.

"So. You ready to get out of here?"

Over the rim of my glass, I squint. When I slam it down on the counter, his broad shoulders shrug up to his ears.

"Excuse me?"

Garret clears his throat just as the faintest shade of pink makes

2

its way up his pale neck and cheeks. "I just figured...well, it's Valentine's Day. And um...I thought you'd be up for something more."

I yank my hand out from under his, then take another deep breath. This time when I exhale, it's slow, measured. There are a million invisible fire ants crawling under my skin, compelling me to toss the rest of my drink in Garret's face for assuming I'd be willing to sleep with him just because it's February fourteenth. Screw that.

"You know something, Garret? You're pathetic. I don't know why you would think I'd be desperate enough to go home with you, especially after I've had to sit here and listen to your bizarre monologue about eating cats and dogs."

I fish a handful of dollar bills from my purse and slam them on the bar. "That's for my drink and tip. Don't leave without paying for your own."

When I stand, I leer at him. This time he's the one leaning away. He's got nowhere to go, though, as the wooden edge of the bar top is digging into his back, blocking his escape.

"For the love of Christ, never, ever speak of pets as food again. It makes you sound like a serial killer."

I yank my purse from the back of my stool before shrugging on my coat. With the fire currently coursing through my veins, I don't even need to wear a jacket. And the single-digit chill outside will do well to cool me off. But taking the time to button my coat gives me a few extra seconds to tear Garret a new asshole.

"Lose my number," I snap. "And if you know what's good for you, don't come back here again. The owner isn't a fan of arrogant pricks like you."

Garret offers nothing in the way of protest. Just silence and a nod. I'm out the door before I can take another breath.

I stand outside on the snow-covered pavement and breathe deep. This winter in Bend, the biggest city in central Oregon, has been a bitch with sub-zero temperatures and record snowfall.

Normally, a heat demon like me would groan at having to stand outside in the icy cold. But it's the perfect opportunity to quell the rage and frustration ravaging my insides. Hopefully these slow, even breaths I'm forcing out will work. Hopefully, that frigid arctic air will take the edge off the fire coursing through me.

I try for a minute, but judging by my racing heartbeat, the sweat beading at the back of my neck, the burn in my eyes, it's an utter fail.

It's not all Garret's fault. The shit-show conversation was all him, but the reason I stand here barely able to keep myself from sobbing on a public street corner is completely on me. I don't know why I thought Valentine's Day would ever be normal again. I should have just stayed home in my pajamas, binged Netflix, and eaten three cartons of Haagen Dazs. Going for a drink at this bar on this night, where one year ago my world turned upside down, was the worst idea I've had in a long time.

Hot tears freeze against my cheeks as the frigid wind whips against me. This day will never, ever be normal again. It will never be anything other than a taunting reminder of my worst heartbreak.

A warm whoosh of air hits the backs of my legs as the door to the bar swings open behind me. Quickly, I wipe my face dry with the back of my mitten-covered hand. The last thing I need tonight is a pitying look from a passing stranger. But there are no foot-steps behind me like I expect. Just the nearby downtown street noise of car honks and snow slushing against tires.

There is a single breath though. One sharp inhale, then a throat clearing. Then my name, spoken by the one person I never, ever thought I'd hear from again.

"Shay?"

I know it's him without even having to turn around and look. The low, whispered tone he employs is so different from how he used to say my name, but I still recognize it. I'd remember that rasp anywhere.

4

"Wes?"

I almost don't believe my eyes when I spin around to look at him. It's been six months since I've laid eyes on him, six months since we've uttered a word to each other. No phone calls, no texts, no form of contact between us for more than one hundred and eighty days. But that sure as hell is him.

That mass of thick brown hair, that smooth tan skin, those earthy brown eyes. The only thing different is his facial hair. What was once the sexiest five o'clock shadow in the universe is now a well-groomed beard.

And his body...damn, that body. Even thick winter clothing can't mar his killer physique. He's still the proud owner of thickly muscled legs and a broad chest. All that traveling must have kept him in killer shape—

Emotion grips me by the throat, and I blink. Drooling over Wes's exquisite body is not allowed. A handful of silent seconds passes, and I'm not tearing up anymore. In fact, all moisture has left my body. My throat is so dry that when I try to speak, I fall into a hacking fit.

He takes a step toward me, but I shake my head. Holding up my hands is my only defense. He gets the message loud and clear because he stays away. I let out a breath, relieved. If he touches me, I might fall to the ground. Or punch him. Hard to say, given how he left things. How he left me.

I whip out my phone and pull up a rideshare app. My apartment is just over a mile away; I could walk. But I need to retreat. Immediately. I can't endure one more minute in Wes's presence, especially after that god-awful date. If I stand here any longer than I have to, there's no telling what I'll do. A car ride home is the fastest way—the best way to protect myself.

I swipe my finger across the screen. The next available car is due to arrive in one minute.

"Shay, are you okay?"

His brows knit together, and my stomach does a backflip. Raw concern paints his face. Everything from the frown lines on his forehead to the purse of his lips conveys that it hurts him to see me like this. Six months ago, I would have handed over one of my organs for that look to flash across his face. That look that says he wants me and nothing else.

Instead, my body reacts differently now. I'm armed with a dry throat and unblinking eyes, struggling to process the fact that Wes Paulsen is standing twelve inches from me.

The phantom taste of tequila hits my tongue. It's spiced oak and smoke and the faintest hint of caramel.

No tequila.

The silent command inside my head is useless. The flavor still dances on my tongue. It was his drink, then mine, then ours. And when he left, it was all I could taste.

It's all I can taste right now.

I sink my teeth into my tongue, letting up just before I draw blood. Now all I taste is fire and acid. No more tequila. Not ever again.

The gray sedan that is my ride pulls up to the curb. For three seconds, I stand between the car and Wes, my eyes darting back and forth between them as if I'm a lost dog who can't remember which one is my rightful guardian.

Wes tugs at the hem of his coat. It's the same black puffer coat he wore the night I met him, a year ago today, in this bar.

"I just...can we talk?" He takes a single step toward me.

The invisible dam inside me breaks. Every word he said the night he left comes flooding back.

I snap out of my haze, blinking back the tears begging to fall down my cheeks. "Stay away from me, Wes."

I jump into the car, slamming the door behind me. I don't turn around to look at him. I don't even peek at the side view mirror to catch a farewell glimpse. I just stare straight ahead, my vision blurry from all the tears.

CHAPTER ONE

Valentine's Day, last year

"*H*ey, Shannon! Shot of Beefeater, will you?"

I glower at the collar-popping frat bro shouting his drink order at my end of the bar. That's the second time this evening that preppy prick has called me the wrong name.

"Listen up, Preppy Prick."

His eyebrows shoot halfway up his forehead. I'm guessing not many people take that tone with this snowflake.

"My name is Shay. I'm here to serve you drinks, but that doesn't mean you get to be an asshole and call me by the wrong name."

The nervous laugh he lets out does little to quell my annoyance. It's ten o'clock on Valentine's Day and for some reason, every single man in Bend has decided to spend his evening camping out at this bar. Possibly because they're aiming to pick up a lonely single lady on the most romantic commercial holiday of the year. That's all well and good, but they still have to treat me with courtesy and respect.

I wave an ice pick at the unblinking douchebag standing inches from me. "What's my name, Preppy Prick?"

He eyes the razor-sharp tip as it glimmers under the low-hanging lights above. The sleek, copper light fixtures are my favorite part of the bar décor. Remy did a hell of a job remodeling this place. He bought it for cheap when it was a run-down industrial space, investing his savings in building it up. Now it boasts an industrial-chic aesthetic that's a hit with pretty much everyone, from hipsters to young professionals to college students. Dark wood furnishings, exposed brick walls, and mood lighting make Dandy Lime a laid-back hangout most nights. Except for tonight when I have to deal with the likes of Preppy Prick.

He stammers out the words. "Your name? Er, um, Shay."

I stab the pick into the block of ice resting on the bar top and drag it across. "I knew you were smarter than you looked. Wanna tell me why you've been calling me Shannon?"

"I um...I don't know." His gaze darts from me to the floor to above my head, then to the side. It's like his brain is playing ping-pong with his eyes.

I bite my lip to keep from laughing. It's hysterical how easy it is to make overconfident pricks like him squirm. All it typically takes is calling them out on their bullshit, giving them a mean nickname, and peppering them with questions. They always, always break.

It's a skill I learned as a kid. Being one of the only mixed-raced kids in school, I got plenty of dismissive and ignorant comments. White kids remarking that I wasn't white enough; Asian kids remarking that I wasn't Asian enough. It was the epitome of ironic, seeing as I'm both. But when I started calling people out, the comments stopped. As I got older, I got bolder, informing any hecklers that if I wanted their worthless opinion on what they thought of me, I'd ask. But I didn't ask them. So I'd tell them to shut the fuck up. They always did.

I employ that same snark and attitude as a twenty-seven-year-old woman. "Well, let me tell you what I know, Preppy Prick. That's your name from now on, by the way, if you order a drink from me ever again." I point to his neck with the ice pick. "That popped collar is atrocious. Fold it down."

"But I—"

"Hey, everyone!" The hum of chatter falls silent as every pair of eyes in the bar turns to me. "Who else thinks this prick should fold down that godforsaken popped collar?"

Every arm shoots up. He obeys with fumbling fingers.

I lean over the counter to him, our faces inches apart. "I may not be a country club cum stain who calls people by the wrong name on purpose like you, but when you're in this bar, you will treat me, every other staff member, and patron with respect. Understand?"

His wordless nod and frantic blinking indicate that he finally gets my drift.

"You said Beefeater, right?"

He nods, still playing eye ping-pong with himself. I pour two shots and slide them to him before swiping the cash from his hand.

A hand taps me on the back. I turn to see Remy beaming at me. "That was a thing of beauty, the way you gave that douche a dressing down."

I shrug. "It was nothing."

"Cuz, it was everything."

He squeezes my shoulder, earning a chuckle from me. Remy and I have the same half-white, half-Filipino background, but he got some Goliath genes on his dad's side. He stands six-foot-three with the build of a linebacker. Utter sweetheart, though, always showering patrons with compliments and praise, always offering hugs and high-fives.

"I just wish you didn't cut back your hours," he says.

"Come on, Remy," I groan. "I need the extra time to focus on my business."

He shakes his head and gives me a side hug. He's the only human being whose side hugs are as cuddly as his full-on ones. I breathe through the squeeze.

"I know. Just thought I'd beg one last time. I'm so proud of you. You know I ordered a print of your latest cityscape water-color, right?"

I smack his arm. "Don't do that! I would have given it to you for free if you just asked."

He shakes his head. "Nope. I want the full customer experience."

I bite back a grin when I think about Remy's sweet gesture. For the past five years, I've slowly built my art business. It was a struggle at first. Trying to make a decent living as a painter-slash-digital artist is no easy task. I've always had to work full-time in office jobs to make ends meet. My paintings and digital prints always generated side money, never enough to justify going full time.

But this past year, I went full force. I created an Etsy shop along with my own website and social media account. I started posting higher quality photos of my work and became more active on Twitter and Instagram. I put out more artwork, more consistently. The result? Three months ago I finally earned enough to quit my soul-sucking job at a local insurance brokerage and focus full time on my shop and artwork. Bartending in the evenings helped me stay afloat, but now I'm making enough that I only have to work a few nights a week at Dandy Lime.

Goosebumps flash across my skin when I think of just how far I've come and how much more I want to accomplish.

Remy hand's fall on his hips. "Now, your prize for being a star employee and verbally kicking Preppy Prick's ass is to take the table in the corner."

He points across the bar to a table of late-twenties men, who are slapping backs and downing shots.

I roll my eyes and suppress a groan. "You're punishing me because I'm cutting back my hours, aren't you?"

"Not at all. They're a little loud, but they've been polite the whole time they've been here. And they've been tipping generously. Have at it."

I perk up at the mention of generous tips and give them my best pageant smile when I clear the empties from their table. "Can I top off anyone's drinks?"

A couple of them ask for refills on their beers, but then a third holds his hand up. "Wait, wait. Can we ask you to do us a favor first? If it's not too much trouble?"

My smile turns tight. I wonder what this "favor" will entail. In the past, when a table full of loud, buzzed guys asks me for a favor, it usually involves my phone number.

"Depends." I rest a hand on my hip. "What's the favor?"

The shaggy-haired guy who asked me the question elbows the man sitting next to him. When my eyes adjust against the dim mood lighting, I have to blink twice. His seat buddy is the dictionary definition of tall, dark, and handsome. At least, I assume he's tall. He's sitting, so I can't say for sure what his height is, but glancing at his long, trouser-clad legs, I'd guess he's got at least handful of inches on my five-foot-seven-inch frame. The rest of the description fits him to a tee, though. His dark hair is cropped short on the sides and runs thick at the top. And his skin boasts a healthy medium-tan that shines under the nearby glow of the overhead copper light fixture.

But it's his stare that's causing the hiccup in my heartbeat, that hitch in my breath. Those burnt umber eyes are kindness and intrigue rolled in one. The moment my gaze hits the warm hue of his stare, I'm falling into a rich hickory abyss.

It's a long second before I realize the shaggy-haired guy is talking again.

"— if you're game." Shaggy smiles. "What do you think?"

"What?"

Shaggy lets out a chuckle. Tall, dark, and handsome's gaze falls to his lap. When he looks back up at me, the faintest rosy hue coats his cheeks.

"Weird request, I know, but Wes here lost a bet. Rules are rules. Think you'd be up for slapping him?"

"You're joking, right?"

Tall, dark, and handsome, aka Wes, shakes his head. "Dead serious."

I roll my eyes. This is a first. Of all the weird and inappropriate requests I've received while serving drinks at my cousin's bar, I've never been asked to physically assault someone. No way I'm starting now.

I play my professionalism card. "Sorry, guys. I'm not in the mood to get fired for assaulting a customer."

I grab more empties with my free hand and walk back to the bar.

"What if we ask your boss?" someone from the table hollers.

"Sure, whatever," I call without looking behind me.

I tend to a few more tables, then feel a tap on my shoulder. Remy smirks at me. "I gave that table my blessing. You can slap that guy if you want."

"Remy, I'm really not in the mood tonight."

"I told them you'll do it for fifty bucks, on top of what they owe you for a tip." Remy peers around me. "If you won't do it, I will. I'd smack around any of those handsome devils for free, actually."

I groan. "Fine." I march back to the table. "Someone order a slap?"

I'm met with soft cheers and fist pumps. This time when I stare at my intended target, something resembling my heart pounds in my chest. I shove away the fleeting giddiness. It's probably the prospect of touching another human being that's sending me into a tizzy. It's been a handful of months since my last date. My last kiss? Months on top of months.

Wes looks up at me, his eyes bright with an undefinable allure I've never seen in anyone else. Their deep hue cuts deep. I wonder if it's possible to freefall into someone's eyes. I give myself a mental smack against the head. He's an attractive man. That's it. Must stop acting like a giddy teenager.

"I'm not going to do this standing up while you're sitting down," I say. "It feels weirdly domineering."

"Fair enough." He stands up, zero evidence of tension on his gorgeous mug. His display of pure ease is in direct opposition to the Ferris wheel of nerves swirling through me.

At full height standing in front of me, I have to tilt my head back to keep my gaze fixed on him. I'd put him a touch above six feet tall.

"Ready?" I ask.

He nods, his eyes never leaving me. One side of his mouth quirks into a half-smile. "Make it good. We've got an audience."

Judging by how the background chatter has softened to whispers, the entire bar is staring at us.

I raise my hand. This handsome stranger with smoky-brown magnets for eyes, this guy named Wes who I feel inexplicably drawn to, doesn't even flinch. Instead, he lets his half-smile widen into a proper full one. That flash of pearly white kills me. I'm about to smack this drop-dead gorgeous man in the face.

I swallow. I rest my palm on his left cheek and it's like my entire hand catches fire. Wes's body is a special kind of warm. The type of warm that makes me want to curl into him and nuzzle his chest, just to see if every other part of him is as deliciously hot as his face.

He leans his face closer. "Just like that. But harder."

On the scale of epic slaps, the one I deliver to Wes's face wouldn't even register. It's nothing like those dramatic ones in the movies. The only reason anyone can hear the noise is because the entire bar has fallen to a self-imposed hush. I didn't have the nerve to pull off anything more than a half-hearted smack. But when my hand falls from his face to my side, the entire bar erupts in cheers and whistles.

The sound barely registers against my eardrums. Instead, all I can focus on is Wes's face. For a split second when my hand made contact with his cheek, he closed his eyes. His smile dropped. But a beat later, he opens his eyes and flashes another heart-melting grin at me, as if I had kissed him instead of struck him.

Against the backdrop of applause in the bar, Wes bows to our audience. When he gestures toward me, I do the same. With everyone turning back to their own tables and conversations, I pivot toward the bar.

"Hey," Wes says from behind me.

I turn around to see his outstretched hand in front of him, that killer smile still on display. "Hell of a way to spend Valentine's Day, right? Thanks for the slap..."

I shake his hand. "Shay," I say, biting back a grin of my own. "My pleasure."

When I let go, I head back behind the bar and dump the nearest bottle of hard alcohol in a shot glass, then down it. Patrón. Not the greatest choice, but it'll have to do. I've never been a big drinker, but I need something, anything to ease me. Every nerve in my body is on high alert after engaging in one of the hottest and most random acts I've ever attempted in my life—with a stranger, no less.

I grab a towel and begin to wipe dry all the freshly washed glasses. It's the perfect mindless activity to keep myself in check. Otherwise, I'd sprint back over to Wes and park myself on his lap, my fingers tugging at that perfect mess of dark hair, teasing his tongue with mine. Now *that* would be unprofessional...and way, way naughtier than that slap.

In my head, the words "hot damn" tumble like a spin-top toy gone rogue.

Holy hot damn is more like. Those moments of eye contact with Wes, the feel of his stubbled cheek under my hand have formed the single hottest moment I've ever experienced on Valentine's Day.

It's not like I haven't had romantic gestures in the past. As a late-twenties single, I've celebrated with dates and boyfriends a handful of times. I've done dinners out, cooked meals in, a couple flower deliveries, even a carriage ride. But they all lacked one thing: heat.

Heat is exactly what's flashed through me ever since making eye contact with Wes minutes ago. And in those minutes since, my body has been roasting, caught in a slow-burn state from the inside out. I swipe my nearly waist-length hair, which is styled in a messy braid, over one shoulder and fan myself. How in the hell can a guy I don't even know make me feel hotter with one look than anyone I've dated in the past?

I touch a damp dishtowel to my face and nearly gasp. The heat from my skin must be seeping through the thick cotton cloth. I can even feel it on my fingertips.

Remy saunters over, fanning himself with a hand.

"I know," I mutter before darting away and down the hall to the bathroom.

Cold water to the face is what I need to snap myself out of these premature hot flashes. I push open the door of the single occupancy women's bathroom just as the person inside of it pulls it open. Losing my balance at the unexpected momentum, I fall forward. Damn it. In my tizzied-up state, I didn't even check to see if the bathroom was occupied.

I tumble forward, but instead of landing the tile floor face-first like I think I will, strong arms brace me, then haul me to a standing position. My fingers dig into what are some very meaty and nicely hairy forearms. The up-close view of red and black flannel registers in my brain. Wes caught me.

When he steadies me back on my feet, I'm pressed against him, my forearms plastered to his chest like we're glued together. We're so close that if I lean my head forward an inch,

I'd graze my forehead against the delicious stubble dotting his chin.

He peers down at me. "You okay?"

Once again, I'm wide-eyed and speechless, all because of that killer stare. I hum "yes" through a breath.

"Sorry," he says. "The men's bathroom was occupied. I already broke the seal and couldn't wait. You know how it goes."

Again I nod, this time my eyes on his lips. So thick and full. I'd give back that fifty-dollar tip for a single bite of that pouty mouth. Clenching my fists, I breathe, somehow keeping my mouth and teeth to myself.

Even through the thick denim of my black skinny jeans, the heat of his touch—his hands on my hips—burns. A hot, delicious burn. Like slowly lowering myself into steamy bathwater.

"Thanks for, um, catching me." I frown up at him, then am immediately distracted by the way his stubbled Adam's apple moves when he swallows. It's another second before I can speak. "I didn't mean to barge in, I—I forgot to check the door, I usually do, I just…"

One corner of his mouth makes that slow journey upward to form a half-smile. "It's okay. Seems like a fitting way to end the evening. Your hand on my face a few minutes ago. You in my arms right now."

The other corner of his mouth curves up, and full-fledged invisible flames consume me. It's decided. Wes is the champion of sexy smiles. He's got the half-smile and the grin in the bag. I'd kill to see a smirk and one with a lip bite.

"I like the way your hands feel on me," he says.

With those words plus his touch and that smile, I'm emboldened. "How about my lips, too?"

When he nods, I press my mouth to his. It's a slow, tentative contact at first. As hot and bothered as I am after endless months of zero kisses, I don't want to drown the poor guy with desperate licks and sucking noises. I set the tone at gentle, nibbling his bottom lip. Another light press of my mouth on his. Then I slide my tongue.

Wes seems to appreciate my measured style because his lips stretch against my mouth in a slow smile. We lick and taste and tease until we're barely able to keep up with the ragged rhythm we've set. When he pulls away, we're both clutching onto the other, gasping for breath.

I rest my forehead against his, staring down at his flannel-clad chest as it heaves up and down. I was mistaken. That slap was just an appetizer. This crazy random, crazy hot kiss in the open doorway of this bar bathroom is what slingshots this Valentine's Day into unforgettable territory. I will never, ever forget this evening when I delivered my first sexy slap, followed by the hottest first kiss I've ever experienced in my life.

"Mmm, Shay…" Wes's gravelly rumble sends electric shocks to my knees. I can barely stand, but it doesn't matter. He's still got me by the waist, propping me up. "Do you—"

"Wes! Where you at, man?"

We both turn our heads in the direction of the booming voice coming from down the hall where we can't see.

"Just uh, gimme a sec, alright?" Wes booms back.

"This is a bar crawl, bro. Chop chop." The voice fades.

We lean away from each other. Wes runs a hand through his wavy hair while I struggle to straighten my hot pink blouse.

"I'm sorry. I…I have to go."

I nod. "Yeah. You should, um, go."

Wes walks out of the bathroom, shutting the door behind him. I lean over the sink and splash icy water against my cheeks, that slap and that kiss looping nonstop inside my head.

CHAPTER TWO

*R*emy closes out the register while I wipe down the bar top. "We did it, cuz! A V-Day for the record books. Can you believe we were that busy?"

"Yeah. Great."

Three hours after Wes left me in a post-kiss tizzy in the women's bathroom and I'm still trapped in a fog of heat and steam. Thinking and speaking are currently off the table until I regain my bearings.

Remy frowns at me. He runs a hand through his short, dark brown hair. "Everything okay with you?"

"Yes. Fine."

He crosses his arms, eyes narrow. "Try again."

I sigh. "Okay, you know that guy you talked me into slapping?"

"The ridiculously sexy and well-groomed lumberjack in the red flannel shirt? Yes, I remember him."

I scrunch the towel between my hands. "We bumped into each other on the way to the bathroom and we sort of, um…kissed."

Remy's jaw plummets to the floor. "And you didn't tell me?"

I explain the awkward run-in that happened by mistake, our hot kiss, and how his friend shouting for him ruined it all.

"Why didn't you get his number?"

"I wasn't thinking straight. It all happened so fast."

"I bet you anything he'll be back here looking for you."

"Let's not get carried away." I turn off the lights in the back.

Remy grabs our coats from the office, and hands mine to me. "You're so pessimistic."

"Realistic," I correct.

He grabs the keys to lock up and we step outside. Arctic air whips across my face, and I pull my beanie down tighter around my ears.

"I'm just saying," Remy says before locking the door. "Have a little faith…"

His words fade into the empty street around us. He points a gloved hand down the block. About ten feet away, Wes stands. My stomach does a backflip.

"See?" Remy elbows me.

Wes walks up to us and shoves his hands in his pockets, his eyes pinning me. "I hope it was okay I surprised you like this."

"Of course." My stomach flutters.

The slight smile he flashes conveys shyness. I freaking adore it.

"I felt bad leaving things the way I did earlier," Wes says. "Would you be up for an early breakfast? I spotted a twenty-four-hour diner down the block. I don't know if it's any good—"

Remy practically shoves me into Wes, who laughs at the obvious move.

"Shay is always starving after a shift. She'd love to go. You couldn't have picked a better diner, my man. Best corned beef hash in the city. Have fun!"

Remy pulls me in for a hug goodbye. "Text me when you get home later, okay?

I nod, appreciative of my cousin's protective streak. He's only a few years older and is well aware that I can look out for myself, but it's comforting to know he cares.

Before he lets me go, he whispers in my ear, "As long as your gut and your lady bits give you the green light, go with it."

I swallow back a laugh just as Remy starts his backward walk shuffle away from us toward his place down the street. He waves goodnight before turning around. Wes and I stand in silence. It's a beat before nerves seep in through the excitement.

"You ready?" he asks.

"Absolutely."

Wes touches the small of my back, leading me in the direction of the diner down the block. An intimate yet respectful gesture. He still gives me enough personal space to walk comfortably at my own pace, unlike most other guys who prefer to crowd around me or grab my hand before I'm ready.

His eyes cut from the quiet street ahead to me. "Hungry?"

"You have no idea."

Wes wags his eyebrows at me over the short stack of blueberry pancakes. "You really think you can beat me?"

"No question." I stab my fork into my short stack of chocolate chip pancakes.

"Shay, you have no idea who you're messing with." He takes an enormous bite before chewing and swallowing. "I've been hiking dozens of miles every day for the past three months. My metabolism is like that of a starving polar bear. You honestly think you can eat more pancakes than me?"

Honest answer? No way in hell. But I'm not admitting that.

Instead, this pancake eating contest is a tactic, a way to stretch this night even longer, this night that's been the most fun date I've ever had.

We talked pleasantries over our first stack of pancakes. I filled him in about how I'm building my art business and working at Remy's bar to help with expenses. Wes shared how he's on month three of hiking across the country, something he's been wanting to do ever since he was a kid. After working as a construction laborer and project manager most of his twenties, he set a goal: save money for a few years, then quit at thirty, drive across the country, and hike scenic spots along the way. He's currently staying with his friend Colin, the tall, shaggy-haired guy from earlier, for the rest of this month to recuperate from his trek in Colorado and to plan the next leg of his trip.

We bonded over our love of electronic dance music and discovered that we both adore the DJ Mari Dash. And now we're indulging in our other mutual love: breakfast food.

"For sure I can eat more pancakes than you." I wink and take another bite.

"It's on." Wes chomps on another forkful and winks back. This is going very, very well.

"Did you eat like this as a kid, too? Good lord."

He swallows. "Pancakes were kind of a treat growing up. I didn't eat them often."

"Impressive. You're certainly making up for it now."

He mock-frowns while swallowing. "I feel one hundred percent confident in my abilities to eat you under the table."

I look up, heat flashing across my cheeks. He's blushing, too. I'm not the only one who picked up on his naughty undertone.

He drops his fork, a flustered chuckle falling from his lips. "That's not...I didn't mean it that way. I'm sorry."

When he finally makes eye contact with me, there's something extra in his stare. It's still just as hypnotic as before, but I could swear I see something else. Something smoldering and hot and fiery, something that says despite his protests, those words are exactly what he wants.

It's exactly what I want, too.

Seeing that fire in his eyes is a comfort. It means we're equally eager to bed each other.

I swallow my last bite and pin him with my stare, prepping

myself to suggest something I've never suggested on a first date before. I speak, my whisper low. "You took the words right out of my mouth. You wanna get out of here?"

The walk to my apartment building would normally take twenty minutes coming from the diner, but with the surge of sugar, carbs, and arousal pulsing through us, we make it in fifteen. That's even with two stops to make out and grope each other along the way.

I've never done the fumbling-kissing-tripping walk home in winter before, and it's much more complicated than in the summer. We're tugging through layers of parka, scarves, and hats. When we tumble all the way to my third-floor studio apartment, we're both sweating and panting.

I don't even bother to flip the light on. I don't want to waste time, and there's no need. Not when streetlights from the outside paint the inside of my apartment in a soft glow.

"First one naked wins," I huff while pulling away from Wes's mouth to shed my boots, beanie, mittens, scarf, and coat.

Wes peels away his winter wear in seconds. He's back in the jeans and flannel I remember from hours ago. He reaches for me, stilling my hands when he softly wraps his fingers around my wrists.

"Let me?"

His touch and his gaze work in unison. I'm rendered immobile by the hypnotic look in his eyes, the heat of his calloused palms on my skin. He pulls me against him, just like he held me when we collided in the bathroom hours ago.

I take a breath to steady myself, the scent of his sandalwood cologne and maple syrup filling my lungs.

"I don't normally do this," I whisper, nuzzling my nose into his chest. I inhale once more.

He buries his face at the top of my head, breathing in through my hair, which has fallen loose from its braid. Thank god I washed it last night.

"I don't ever do this," he chuckles.

"Yeah, right." A guy who looks like him must be fighting off women constantly.

"I'm serious, Shay."

His gentle grip slides to my shoulder. He tilts me back to look down at me. "Look, I don't mean to freak you out, but I've never hit it off like this with someone before. I've only known you for an evening, but I really like you. Something about you…" His gaze falls to my neck, my chest, my mouth, then he makes that slow trail back up to my eyes. "Something about you sets me at ease. I noticed it from the get-go, from the moment you stood next to me. And I just…I just want to go with the flow as long as you want to."

The heat coursing inside me turns to flames. When I press my lips to his, it's as if no time has passed since our heated kiss in the bathroom hours ago.

With his hands on either side of my face, he pulls me away, breaking our kiss. We both pause to gasp.

"So you feel it too?" he asks.

"One hundred percent."

I push him across the open space of my studio apartment. He walks backward until the backs of his knees hit the edge of my bed and he falls into a sitting position. Standing over him, I pull my blouse over my head.

Wes's brow flies up his forehead. "Holy shit…"

Soft, slow-moving hands skim up my torso, stopping at the cups of my bra. When his fingers begin to massage, my head falls back in a moan. I brace myself with my hands on his shoulders.

"You're gorgeous." He moans the words, his mouth pressed against my belly.

He kisses upward, the trail marked by the moisture of his tongue and lips. My bra is on the floor before I even register that he's unlatched it.

One swirl of his tongue around my nipple and I'm gasping.

The light scrape of his teeth along the soft skin right under my boob sends my hands to his hair. I try to only give him a light tug, but I fail. I can't help it. Maintaining total control is impossible against Wes's mouth.

"You liked to be teased?" he whispers.

I nod down at him. I can only imagine what I must look like, my mouth half-open, my bare chest heaving, my face in what feels like a pleading frown, aching for more.

Without another word, he repeats the same teasing licks, the same teasing scrapes over my other breast. Counting the seconds is the only way I don't faint. Every slow, wet maneuver of his tongue sends heat to every sensitive spot on my body. Between my legs, I'm throbbing. Every pulse is an ache for release. I need his hand, his cock, his mouth, his anything there very, very soon.

His lips fall away from my skin as he unzips my jeans. "This is okay?" he asks while looking up at me.

He doesn't move another inch until I nod my approval. The slow fall of denim reveals cotton hipster panties. Wes greets my bare thigh with light kisses, whispering how much he loves the sight before him.

Then he trails that killer mouth from the tops of my thighs to the insides. His kisses are downright addictive. The perfect balance of firmness and softness. And wetness. His tongue...oh boy, his tongue. Wes has perfected the art of tantalizing licks.

When the top of his head grazes the crotch of my panties in the middle of yet another inner thigh kiss, my knees buckle. Just the whisper of contact and I'm a wreck.

"Wes," I moan. "I can't stay standing much longer."

He's on his feet a half-second later, holding me up with his arms, his chest against my chest. Thank heavens I've got his body to lean on. That look on his face, it's almost menacing. Those dark dilated eyes, those hooded lids, his mouth a straight line. That look conveys intensity, hunger, need. The perfect trio. It's enough to melt me into a puddle on the hardwood floor beneath me.

I clutch his shoulders with the tenacity of a baby koala. And then that half-smile reappears.

"Good thing you don't need to be standing for what I'm about to do," he growls.

He pivots, lowering me to the bed. On my back, I clutch my bedsheets, staring up at the darkened ceiling.

It's the hook of his thumbs over the hem of my panties that causes my first gasp. They hit the floor, pooling at the tops of my feet before I can even inhale. The soft, light swirl of his tongue is the cause of my second one. And another gasp, and another. The motion never stops. It's slow and steady, then fast and hard. Then he dials back a notch to even and slow. The entire time I'm panting, begging, moaning.

When his cheeks slide against the insides of my thighs, my lids fly open and I have to silently tell myself not to scream. That combination of sensations—the hard scrape from his stubble mixed with the soft warmth of his tongue—has my brain in a tizzy.

I ask for more, harder, faster, then slower. He listens and follows, like a star pupil that takes direction perfectly.

I groan, then he groans, the vibrations pulsing through my thighs and up my midsection. Chomping down on my lip is the only way I can keep from shouting like a rabid banshee. This pleasure, this heat, this buildup, it's all too much. I will most certainly explode into a million unrecognizable pieces when he sends me over the edge.

Every lick and lap winds me tighter and tighter.

"Fuck," I gasp, one hand tangled in his hair, the other tangled in the sheets.

He pauses, lifting his head up from between my legs, licks his lips, and smirks. "In a second."

The moment he resumes, I'm gone. Climax rips through me, taking my body with it. Every muscle in me cramps, every inch of me thrashes against the mattress. I cry out, but it's nothing sensible, nothing that can be considered words. Just screams and moans and gasps.

But Wes seems to understand me perfectly. It's in that satisfied stare he flashes me, that taunting half-smile that quickly turns into a Cheshire cat grin. And then I know it's finally my turn.

Pushing myself up to a sitting position, I claw at his flannel shirt.

He chuckles, slowing my hands by placing his on top of mine. "Buttons, remember?"

I laugh an embarrassed "sorry," but he places his index finger under my chin and presses a soft kiss to my mouth.

"Don't apologize. Do you have any idea how hot it is to have you clawing at me?"

His shirt lands on the floor. He leans up to take his pants off while I flip on my bedside lamp.

"Wait." I still him with a hand on his forearm. "I just want to…" My hands finish for me. I run my palm against the mass of lines and muscle that is his upper body. Tracing my index finger along the lines of his stomach earns me a soft laugh.

He squints down at me. "Have I passed inspection?"

"With flying colors. Hiking gets you pretty ripped, huh?"

Wes shrugs. "I wanted to get into shape for my trip."

"You sure did. Nicely done."

I press the pads of my fingers against each of his abs. So, so many abs.

Leaning forward, I press a feathery-soft peck against the left half of his Adonis belt. His breath catches above me. I reach over to the drawer of my nightstand and tear a condom from the packet I bought months ago.

When I turn back to him, I blink. Judging by the generous bulge under those gray striped boxers, I'm in for one hell of a good time.

"May I?" I ask.

26

Flushed cheeks flank his close-lipped smile when he nods. When I pull down his boxers, I'm the one flushing.

"Am I glad I met you," I say.

He chuckles, his eyes shy. But when I slide my tongue over his tip, the chuckling soon turns to grunts.

"Shay. Fuck…" Wes hisses as I lick up and down.

I'm not skilled enough to take all of him fully in my mouth, but he doesn't seem to mind. What I manage with my mouth and my hand seems to satisfy judging by the way he groans and the way his hand grips my shoulder for dear life.

Soon he pulls me off and gently pushes me back down on the bed. Swiping the condom from my hand, he rips it open with his teeth, then slides it on. He hovers over me, and I'm flanked on either side by sculpted arms. I'm tempted to lean up so I can lick and bite him, but he holds either side of my head between his palms.

"That was incredible, but I want this. Is that okay?"

Enthusiastic nodding is my answer. When he slides in, my jaw falls open. A breathy howl escapes me. That size and that girth are a hell of a combination.

I gasp for air. "How…how do you feel so good?"

It's a silly question, but my mind is pleasure-mush, unable to process anything other than thrusts and heat. Well-worded questions are a no-go.

"Funny," he grunts. "I was just about to ask you the same thing."

We both laugh, then moan in unison. I'm back to my commands of harder, slower, faster, more. Every slide, every thrust is heaven on my body.

When he laces his fingers in mine, pressing them against the mattress, my breath catches. Yes. This is exactly how I want to come, his hands gripping me, face-to-face, our bodies molded together.

I've never, ever been one to climax the first time I'm with a guy. But tonight is different. Anything is possible with a well-endowed almost-stranger I feel instant chemistry with.

The friction from his pelvis rubbing against my most sensitive spot has me seeing stars already. "I'm close," I whisper.

"Me too."

Friction gives way to heat, which gives way to climax for the second time in one night. My body moves just the same. Thrashing, convulsing, shaking. Only this time it's done while I'm wrapped around Wes. Sweet, solid, intoxicating Wes.

He grunts and tenses above me, then eases. We end with him on top of me, a perfect pile of sweat, skin, and breath.

It's a struggle just to mumble with my brain coated in post-pleasure fog, my body a trembling mass. But somehow the words spill out. "Best. Valentine's Day. Ever," I gasp.

A throaty laugh and a kiss on my forehead are his replies. "You took the words right out of my mouth."

CHAPTER THREE

*G*entle scratches on my shoulder wake me. It's Wes's stubble as he softly kisses me. I give a satisfied "Mmm," then yawn.

I register his body spooned against me. So that must be why I feel so toasty. Most winter mornings I cocoon myself into my comforter like a human burrito. But this morning I don't have to, with Wes's skin on my skin creating the most delicious heat. What a delightful change of pace.

He kisses a trail along the side of my neck before hugging me from behind. I groan at his slow, steady pace. Already my heart is racing. The ease in which we wake up in each other's arms is almost unnerving. How can I feel so comfortable with someone I met less than twenty-four hours ago?

Remy's words from last night echo in my brain.

As long as your gut and your lady bits give you the green light, go with it.

"Good morning," Wes says, his voice low and scratchy.

I spin around, offering my own greeting in the form of a sloppy, teasing kiss. My gut and my lady bits are still very, very into Wes.

"One sec," he mutters between kisses before jetting off to the bathroom.

When he walks back out, he stops at the makeshift office space I have set up in the corner of my studio apartment. I fight the urge to cover my face with a pillow. He's getting an up-close look at the cluttered mess I call my dream job.

I watch him as his gaze moves slowly across my workspace. Watercolors, colored pencils, and oil pastels scatter the surface. A pile of blank canvases rests on the floor. A trio of watercolor portraits I've been commissioned to do hang on the walls as they dry. He walks up to my easel in the corner, which houses my latest work: a watercolor cityscape at twilight. Hues of purple and blue splash across the center of the canvas. He squints, I assume at the hefty amount of white space bordering the image.

"It's not done yet," I croak.

The way he beams at me settles me instantly. "It's gorgeous. Absolutely stunning."

He crawls back into bed with me, moving so his back is against the headboard, then cuddles me against him. In this position, we have a head-on view of my art space.

"I didn't know you also did portraits," he says, pointing at the portrait sitting on my easel. "They're breathtaking."

I study the half-finished rendering of a client's wife. An anniversary gift. I glance down at our arms laced together. It's so natural, sitting like this.

"That's sweet of you to say, thank you." I let my head fall back against his shoulder. "They're my favorite things to work on, next to watercolor cityscapes. I wish I could do them more often, but I only do portraits when people submit a request on my website for one, which is only every couple of months."

Wes must have some sort of superhuman ability to set strangers at ease. I feel like I'm chatting with my best friend or family when I talk to him.

"You're an incredibly talented artist."

"Trying to be."

He pats my hand. "Don't talk yourself down. You're brilliant, and it's obvious. And given you're building a business, you're clearly kicking ass."

"I have to work nights at my cousin's bar to keep up with my bills. That's hardly kicking ass."

"Hey." The stare he flashes is a no-nonsense brand of seriousness. "Don't say that. You're working hard to make your dream come true. In a world where millions of people work jobs they hate, that's the very definition of kicking ass."

I let a smile loose, basking in his heartfelt praise. "My parents say the exact same thing."

"See? I know what I'm talking about." He settles back behind me.

"That must be a go-to thing for all parents to say if yours and mine say it," I chuckle.

The muscles in his stomach tighten against my back. He clears his throat. "Fun plans today?" he asks, his lips pressed against the back of my neck.

"I promised Remy I'd stop by the bar this afternoon and help take down the Valentine's decorations."

"What are you doing until then?"

"Not a whole lot."

"Could I maybe keep you company until you have to go?" He skims a finger along the curve of my hip before letting his hand settle between my thighs.

"I would love that."

~

THE WALK to Dandy Lime is a challenge and not just because of the beard burn on my thighs.

It's because I'm fighting the urge to grab Wes by the hand, march him back to my apartment, and dive right back into bed. I smile to myself, my mind replaying the pornographic film reel of this morning and afternoon spent entirely in my bed. Wes and I didn't leave my mattress until the last possible moment, when I had thirty minutes to shower and walk to work.

Even with the raw thighs and the wet hair in single-digit temperatures that will surely give me pneumonia, I can only think of one word: *more.* I want more sweet smiles, more easy conversation, more of that magnetic feeling.

I want more Wes.

But I can't say that. That would make me sound unbelievably desperate. So instead, I just keep walking.

Wes wags an eyebrow at me. "So that was fun."

"It was." I beam at the sidewalk.

We stop outside the entrance of the bar. Both of us do our own versions of nervous shuffling. Wes shoves his hands in his coat pockets while squinting at the surroundings; I cross my arms and stare at the ground.

I bite back all the questions I want to ask. Will he be busy during his month-long pit-stop in the city? Does he want to see me again? Is he as blown away as I am that we've hit it off so well, so fast?

Saying any of that would be a major faux pas. I'm the one who asked him to my place last night. I made the last major move, and to initiate the next one could make me look too eager.

I swallow back all the words dancing on the tip of my tongue. No more overthinking. Just relax and play it cool.

"Thanks for walking me," I say.

"Of course." He offers a gentle smile before taking a step toward me.

A long beat of silence follows. He says nothing; I say nothing.

Finally, mercifully, he speaks. "Shay, would you—"

His phone ringing interrupts him. I grit my teeth, fighting the urge to snatch it out of his hand and toss it into a nearby sewer grate. What awful, no good, very bad timing. Instead, I stand quietly and pretend to check something on my phone while he finishes his conversation.

"They what? When?" A concerned frown cloud's Wes's face. "Shoot, yeah. Hang on, man. I'm coming."

When he hangs up, his frown says everything. He will not be asking me out.

"Sorry, my friend Colin—the shaggy-haired guy from last night—he needs my help. I gotta run."

"Oh um, sure..."

He spins around and jogs away before I can even mutter "bye."

I'm disappointed even though I have no right to be. We had an epic one-night stand that turned into morning and afternoon sex. That's better than what most people get when they hook up with a stranger. It's not fair to expect anything more.

Remy's beaming face greets me when I walk into the bar.

"So your gut and your lady bits had fun last night, I take it?"

I roll my eyes. "Good afternoon to you too." I start swiping origami hearts from the tables.

Remy rounds the edge of one, armed with a giddy smile. "Come on, tell me everything!"

"There's nothing to tell."

Remy stares me down, hands on his hips. "That's some bullshit if I've ever heard it. It's three in the afternoon. You're sporting a wet ponytail *and* he walked you here. You had a hell of a time. Spill."

I roll my eyes. "We had a nice night and morning and afternoon. After he walked me here, he got a panicked phone call from his friend and then took off."

"That's it?" Remy frowns.

"That's it." I tug down the construction paper hearts hanging from the ceiling. "Nothing else to say."

"No asking for your number? No plans to meet up later?"

I turn away from Remy and toss the hearts in a nearby cardboard box. I'm so not in the mood for an interrogation from my well-meaning cousin.

Even in the silence, I can hear the gears in Remy's head turning. He pats my shoulder. "He'll be back, don't you worry."

I scoff at the confidence in his tone. "I won't be seeing him anytime soon, Remy."

I weave through the tables, picking up the leftover dishes of candy hearts from the bar top, Remy trailing behind me.

"He's into you whether you see it or not."

I try not to roll my eyes. If there's one thing more bothersome than a disappointing end to a date, it's the pep talk loved ones give you afterward to try and help you feel better.

"Look, I don't know much, but I know that a guy wouldn't wait outside a bar at one in the morning when it's cold as hell to ask a woman out unless he felt something strong." Remy's hands fall on his hips. "I guarantee he was going to ask you out, but the surprise phone call tripped him up." He tosses a handful of decorations into a box. "He'll be back. Mark my words."

I swallow back a groan. "Can we drop it?

He holds his palms up to me. "Fine."

I head to the back office to grab the step ladder so I can take down the pink streamers in the back hallway.

Remy's hollered voice follows me all the way. "You know I'm right, cuz."

In the privacy of the office, I let out the annoyed groan I've been holding in. "Fat chance," I mutter.

CHAPTER FOUR

Two hours till closing time the day after Valentine's Day and Dandy Lime has hit a pleasant, steady rhythm. Not slammed, but not slow. Customers have been polite and generous in their tips. Remy hasn't had to frog-march any drunken patrons out the door.

He walks up to the bar and asks for a tray of sex on the beaches. "Twenty-first birthday." He gestures to the lively group of young ladies in the back corner. "You know how it goes."

I mix the drinks. Remy picks up the loaded tray before something at the entrance catches his eye. And then he grins, leaning down to my ear. "Romeo's back. Told you."

I spin around faster than I mean to, and I have to grip the counter to keep from falling over. Heat flashes across my skin when I see Wes's smiling face. He takes a free seat at the bar, the one right in front of me.

"What a surprise." Somehow my tone is easy, casual. A miracle considering the somersaults in my stomach.

He glances down at the bar top where his hand rests. He runs his other hand through his hair. "Sorry for how I left this afternoon. Colin's car got broken into and he was in a panic when he called me for help."

"That's awful. Is everything okay?" I rest my hand on top of his. The warmth of his skin on my skin is divine.

"It will be. Just a long day of filing police reports and dealing with insurance."

"You want a drink? Sounds like you could use one."

"Got any good tequila?"

"Best we've got is Patrón Reposada."

He makes a "not bad" face. "Better than I expected."

I playfully smack his hand before filling a glass. He takes a long sip while I check on the couple seated next to him.

Wes tips his glass to me as if he's toasting me. "From now on, whenever I drink good tequila, I'll think of you. That's a damn good pour you gave me. Perfect amount of ice, too."

Biting my lip, I glance down, thankful for how my tan skin conceals the heat flashing through me. If I were pale, my red cheeks would be visible from outer space.

"I can do more than just paint pretty pictures."

"That you can, Shay."

That familiar flash ignites in his eyes, the same look that pinned me in my bed last night, this morning, and this afternoon. It feels like we're the only two people in this bar.

He sets his glass on the counter. "Look, I know the standard thing is to play it cool and not seem too eager, but I really like you."

Slowly, I exhale. It's bliss hearing him say that.

"I'm here for a month, and I'd like to see you as much as I can while I'm here," he says. "If you're interested."

I am a nodding, smiling fool. "I'd love that."

He downs the rest of his glass, then stretches his arm out to my face, tucking a stray chunk of hair behind my ear. "Text me after you're done here. Maybe we can grab breakfast again."

"Or you can meet me at my place?"

He smiles. "That works too."

Leaning forward, he kisses me. It's decidedly PG, nowhere near the wild, X-rated kisses of last night or this morning. We're in public after all. But it's still one hundred percent hot. Anything having to do with Wes's mouth on me is hot.

He pays, we say goodbye, and he heads out the door.

"What did I tell you, cuz?" Remy pulls me into a bear hug from behind.

I tap his arm and he finally releases me. "Fine, you were right."

"You two are so damn precious already."

I shove his arm, but his solid frame doesn't budge. "He's only here for a month. We're just having a good time. Don't get carried away."

Remy flashes me his best "yeah right" face. "You invited him to your place tonight. For the second night in a row. I'd say that's veering near 'carried away' territory. You're smitten."

I toss a tea towel at him, but he catches it easily with one hand. I roll my eyes and bite back the smile aching to spread across my face. Because Remy's right. I'm smitten for sure.

~

THREE WEEKS into Wes's "I'd like to see you as much as I can" proposal, and the two of us have sprinted yards past the "smitten" boundary.

We've seen each other every single day since the night he surprised me at Dandy Lime. If I'm working a bar shift, he'll come in an hour before close and nurse a tequila on the rocks while waiting for me. If I'm free, we grab dinner or a drink. If I'm working from home, he stops by my apartment, always with a meal packed for us to share. There is always sex. Never has there ever been a more enjoyable three weeks on this planet.

I'm constantly smiling, giddy, laughing. Remy comments every time he sees me. That I seem like I'm floating on a post-orgasmic cloud 24/7. I brush it off, but he's right. I am obnoxiously happy. And it's different from the joy I've experienced with the guys I've been with in the past. Every time I see Wes, my stomach flips, my heart skips, my breath catches. One look at him, and it's like a beam of sunlight explodes from within me. Simply being around him—cuddled together in my bed, watching Netflix on my couch, holding hands while walking down the street—is an unfamiliar, all-encompassing contentment I've never known before.

I stare at the most recent work on my easel. The image smiling back at me is evidence of just how different these feelings and these past few weeks with Wes have been.

Against the stark white of the canvas, a charcoal rendering of his face half-smiles back at me. With my fingers, I smudge the mass of black that is his hair. Then I take the pencil, darkening in his eyes. When I finish, I lean back and study it. Heat glides up my neck and cheeks. After a second, I roll my eyes. It's a sketch of him and yet I'm as giddy as if he were standing here in front of me, displaying that panty-dropping grin.

I've never once drawn a guy I've dated before. The thought's never crossed my mind. But with Wes, it's different. Everything is, from the way my hand tingles when he holds it, to the safety I feel when I fall asleep in his arms. It's a feeling that's grown ever since the night we agreed to see where things could go during his time here. Now it's full-fledged emotions linking me to him.

I scan the floor, where a handful of watercolor paintings I've done of Wes lay, drying in the patch of sunlight streaming in through the window.

A knock at my door makes me jump.

"Just a sec!"

I flip over the canvas on my easel so the image faces the wall. With careful hands, I check the paintings. Dry, thankfully. I scramble to stack them together and tuck them behind the canvas on the easel. I take slow, deep breaths, the evidence of my growing feelings hidden safely away.

When I open the door, Wes stands, cloth bag in hand. "Thought you might want a little something to eat before your shift tonight."

I thank him and step aside to let him in. We kiss, plop on my couch, and dig into the turkey club sandwiches he so lovingly made.

"Avocado?" I say around a bite. "What did I do to deserve such luxury? That stuff's expensive."

He kisses the tip of my nose before taking a bite. "You mentioned the other day that you gave it up to save money. Thought you deserved a treat."

While chewing I nuzzle his neck, then sink my back against his chest.

"How's work going?" Wes asks.

"Good. Busy, which I love. A guy hired me to illustrate a storybook of his first date with his girlfriend. It's a gift for her birthday next month. Super romantic."

Wes finishes one half of the sandwich, then swipes the other half from the coffee table. I dig into the container of carrot sticks.

"Now how the hell are the rest of us supposed to measure up to a romantic gesture like that?" he says.

I snuggle closer to him. "I think you're doing pretty well."

We finish our sandwiches and he takes our trash to the kitchen. On his way back to the couch, he halts at my desk. He hunches over, staring at the illustrations I'm working on for the book.

"Damn, Shay. These are fantastic."

He runs a finger over the edge of the paper, careful to avoid the actual images. I smile at his mindfulness. I mentioned the first week we started spending time together that smudges are the bane of my existence, so I always set down tissue paper under my hand when I draw.

I walk over to him and flip the pages over so he can see the rest.

"Disneyland was their first date," I say. "Epic, right?"

Wes's eyes cut to me, and I have to remind myself to breathe. It's the exact same stare I captured in my charcoal drawing. It draws out the exact same reaction from me. Proof that no matter if he's on paper or in person, he absolutely does it for me.

He winks. "Not as epic as ours. You can't get much better than a slap in the face followed by making out in the bathroom."

I shove his arm, and he reaches for the side of my stomach, tickling me until I squeal. Instinctively I jump back, bumping my easel.

A thud on the floor makes the two of us turn around. There lie my charcoal painting and every single watercolor work I've done of Wes, all of them face up.

My hands fly up to cup my mouth. The gesture does little to muffle my choked gasp. I take a step toward the sheet nearest me, but it's too late. Wes is kneeling on the floor, a watercolor of his face in his hand, examining it with a narrow stare. He's like a scientist studying bacteria growth on a petri dish.

"What's all this?" he asks.

I stand over him, shuffling back and forth on my bare feet. I must look like I have to pee.

"It's um…nothing."

That's the most pathetic excuse I could have come up with, especially when the truth is so obvious.

He frowns at the watercolor, then twists his head to the charcoal lying on the floor just a few inches away. "These are me?"

His face goes pale.

"Yes."

"Wow. Okay."

Judging by the stunned look on his face and how he says nothing else for several seconds, he is not flattered. He is shocked and terrified.

When he finally turns to me, he doesn't even look at me. He just grabs his coat and scurries out the door.

Stunned, all I can do is stand and stare at the door. It's official. I've solidified my status as a creepy artist who spends my free time drawing the guy I'm sleeping with. I've sprinted past the admirer category. I am the queen of the stalkers.

I look over at the scattered artwork on the floor once more. From this angle, it looks like a creepy mosaic. I walk over, stack the drawings, and shove them under my desk. Tangling both hands in my hair, I blink back tears. In ten minutes, I ruined everything between us.

CHAPTER FIVE

"Four shots of tequila, please." The college-aged hipster doesn't smile when he speaks or hands over the cash in his hand.

Good. I don't think I could take a smile on top of his drink order. Just the mention of tequila reminds me of the one person I shouldn't be thinking about.

Four days since Wes discovered my stash of sketches and paintings, and we haven't spoken. No calls or texts from me, of course. No way in hell am I initiating contact after what I've done.

He hasn't reached out, either.

I thought leaving the ball in his court would be best. He's the one who's had to process the shock and surprise. He needs time to think, to decide what to do next.

I was hoping for at least a *We should talk* text, but not even that. As terribly as that conversation would most certainly go, it would be better than the limbo I live in now, where I don't know where we stand, where my feelings track up and down every hour of every day like I'm riding an out-of-control roller coaster.

I hand the hipster his change. He says a quiet "thanks" before taking the shots to his table.

Remy saunters up next to me while I wipe a towel over the surface. "Romeo hasn't been in for a while. What's up with that?"

"I don't think he'll be coming back. Ever," I mutter.

Remy gently grips me by the arm and leads me to the end of the bar where there are no customers. "What are you talking about?"

I cross my arms, my eyes refusing to look anywhere than the floor. "I'm pretty sure I screwed up everything."

"You two have an argument or something?"

"I wish."

There's at least a playbook for making up after an argument. Storming out, cooling off, a night of fitful sleep. Then someone bites the bullet and is the first to call or text. Apologies are exchanged. Then copious amounts of makeup sex ensue.

There is zero guidance for what to do when the person you're dating stumbles upon a stash of stalker artwork you've made of them.

I look around the bar to make sure no one is paying attention to our conversation. "I've been doing drawings of him ever since we got together."

Remy frowns. "And?"

I bury my face in my hands. "I did, like, six drawings and paintings of him. I didn't tell him about it because I didn't want to look like a creep, drawing him in my spare time. So I hid them behind the canvas on my easel." I heave a breath. "He came over to surprise me with lunch the other day, and I bumped into the easel, knocking over every single one of my drawings. They landed face-up all over the floor. And he saw them. All of them."

Remy makes a wincing noise through his teeth. "Yeah, that's..."

I jerk my head up, my hands falling to my side. "Something a maniac would do, yes. I know."

He grimaces. "Maybe he thought it was flattering?"

"I was standing there, watching him look at all the pictures. He was definitely not flattered. Shocked and horrified is more

43

like it. He muttered 'wow,' then left. I haven't heard from him since."

Remy stutters for a good five seconds.

"The look on his face." I groan. "He thinks I'm nuts, no question."

A group of businessmen barges in, cackling loudly while making their way to the bar.

Remy gives my hand a squeeze. "We'll talk more later."

I nod at him before taking a breath so I can make it through the end of my shift.

REMY WRAPS his arm around me as we close in on our apartment building after our shift.

"Don't beat yourself up about this whole thing. What you did was sweet. If he can't see that then…"

Remy stills in his tracks. I look up to see what's distracting him and immediately lose my breath. There's Wes, standing at the door of our apartment building.

"Oh damn," Remy mumbles.

When Wes looks up, his gaze locks on mine. He offers a soft smile that reads more apologetic than anything. I take a breath, steadying myself. This must be it. He's finally coming to end it.

We walk up to the door.

"Hey," he says, his eyes darting between me and Remy.

"Wes. How's it going?" He pulls me into a hug. "Stay strong. Call me later if you need anything."

I nod into his shoulder. Remy walks into the building to his first-floor apartment. I turn back to Wes.

He flashes an unsure expression. "Can we talk?"

"Sure."

The walk upstairs to my place is silent. When we're inside, we shed our coats and shoes, then he settles on the couch.

"Something to drink?" I ask while walking into the kitchen.

"Um, okay."

I have to close my eyes and grip the counter. Wes's voice sounds so shaky. He must be so nervous about what he's going to say to me. But then I swallow, open my eyes, and stand straight. This is just the way things go sometimes. I need to be an adult and accept it.

I grab the nearly full bottle of Dulce Vida tequila from my cabinet. It was a gift from Remy when I decided to go full-time with my art business. We took one shot together in celebration, then I stored it away.

With two glasses in my other hand, I carry it all to the couch and set them on the coffee table. When I sit down next to him, I make sure I'm giving him enough space. Even though everything in me aches to cuddle into him, that's not appropriate. Not if he's going to break up with me.

He stares down at his lap, his eyebrows knit. "I wanted to talk to you about..." He gestures to the space under my desk, where my drawings and paintings of him sit in a neat stack. Worst hiding spot ever.

"Right."

I pour us both glasses. We take quiet sips. I swallow, then sip again. The burn finally fades, leaving behind warmth.

I clear my throat and turn to him. "Look, I know what you must be thinking—"

He grabs my hand. "I love that you drew me." His words are like a glass of cold water after a crawl through the desert.

"You...you do?"

"Absolutely. I was just surprised at first because I figured it meant you felt something deep for me." He pauses. "And I figured it meant we feel the same way about each other—because I feel something deep for you, Shay."

"That's exactly how I feel." My heart races when I finally admit it out loud.

"I was just shocked in the moment, that's why I left," he says. "I couldn't believe we felt the same way about each other. It was like it was too good to be true and I needed a minute to process it all."

The sharp inhale I take through my open mouth nearly makes me cough.

"I've felt a connection with you from the get-go." He raises his brow, and it's the first hint of uncertainty I've seen in him all night. "I think you have, too?"

"Obviously." A chuckle falls from my mouth. "I was drawing and painting pictures of you."

He beams and leans over to cup my cheek in his hand. I let out a soft moan, holding my hand over his. We lower our hands to the space between us, our fingers intertwined.

Wes's eyes bore into me. "I want to stay here in Bend for a while. I want to give us a shot, Shay."

His last word is barely out before I lunge for him. My mouth is on his mouth before he can even wrap both arms around me.

"I want that too," I say between kisses.

A million questions fly through my mind: What about the hike across the country he's planned for so long? What will he do for work? Where will he live?

But every kiss erases those questions. Soon my mind and my body are filled with just him. My brain, my heart, can't process anything else. Details don't matter. Right now, we're together. We're giving this—we're giving *us*—a proper shot. I don't care about anything else.

CHAPTER SIX

"*Y*ou ready for your surprise?" Wes navigates my car around a sharp curve of highway.

"I'm ready," I say.

Two months into Wes's extended stay and we're finally making it out to the nearby mountains for a hike. Ever since he made the decision to stay, he hasn't been able to do much outdoor stuff. He's been busy working and getting settled into his new living quarters: my apartment.

Gazing out the window, I smile to myself. Life details were easier to work out than expected. Finding work was easy. Colin hired him on as a project manager at his construction company and even offered to let him stay at his place. That wasn't necessary, though, because I offered up my place the morning after our mutual confession of shared feelings.

Remy warned it might be a disaster to move in this soon, but it's the one time he's been wrong so far. Every day has been a dream. Waking up to the person you're head over heels for, falling asleep cuddled into their perfect crook of an arm, is the exact opposite of a disaster. It's the greatest feeling on Earth.

Wes pulls the car into a snowpark off the highway. During the winter months, people park here, then cross country ski along the nearby trails. Since it's spring, there's still snow on the ground, but enough has melted to do a short hike.

When we jump out of the car, Wes heads to the trunk, opens it, and pulls out my sketchpad and colored pencils.

"I've never seen you sketch a wilderness scene before," he says. "I was hoping you could try that today."

He leads me down the trail, which follows a creek. A half-mile later, we hit a waterfall. He points to a massive boulder sitting near the edge of the creek, just below the waterfall.

"How's this for a spot to sketch?" he asks.

"Perfect."

We sit side by side, and for an hour I sketch while Wes takes photos, then sits silently, gazing at the scenery around us. Behind the lush evergreen tree line sit majestic mountains, their peaks still coated in snow. It's the exact scene I'm trying to capture in my signature style: the image in the center, taking up about two-thirds of the white space. The remaining white space that surrounds the image serves as an imaginary frame to make the image in the middle pop.

When I finish, he leans over to take a look. I could swear his eyes sparkle when they scan the paper. "Incredible." He kisses my forehead.

I hold up the sketch, the scenery that inspired my drawing directly behind it, and take a photo on my phone so I can post it on my Instagram account later tonight. Since February, I've doubled the visits to my website. I've been commissioned to paint a handful of portraits, and last month I was hired to illustrate a children's book. That will be a long-term project with multiple rounds of revisions and could lead to more illustration work. Plus, my digital designs and watercolor landscapes have been selling steadily on my website, too.

My stomach still takes a tumble whenever I see glowing comments on my site or my work trending on social media. It really does feel like my career as an artist is taking off, and I'm more inspired than ever.

The most exciting part? Wes's portraits are bestsellers. After he gushed about them, he suggested I sell them. When I listed them, every single one of them sold—except for the charcoal one, my favorite, and one of the watercolors, which I want to keep for myself.

He packs my sketch pad in his backpack, handling it carefully as if it's his most prized possession. I have to look away, I'm so taken aback. No guy has ever shown this level of thoughtfulness for my work before. We hike a quarter-mile up the trail to another waterfall. I sketch some more, he takes more photos, and we head back to the car.

On the drive home, my phone rings.

"Hang on, it's my mom."

When I answer, she immediately dives into an unclear and rambling question about her computer.

"*Anakko*, I tried to skip your brother, but it won't turn on."

Technology and my mother are long-time foes. Ever since I was a little kid, she's always had an impossible time working anything with a battery or an electrical cord.

"You mean Skype, Mom."

She sighs. "Yes, Skype. That's what I said. Okay, so I keep trying to skip your brother, but I just keep recording videos of myself. I don't know what I'm doing wrong."

I bite my lip to keep from laughing. "You're in the wrong program. Click on that blue icon with the white 'S' in the middle."

"Icon?" She's definitely frowning, her face an inch from her giant computer screen.

"Mom, just look at the computer screen. Then look at the left half toward the bottom. See the big 'S' I was talking about?"

Silence follows, then she hums. "It's not there."

I swallow back a groan. I love her to the moon and back, but talking her through a technology-related task requires a heroic level of patience I don't possess.

"You'll have to do a search for it then."

"A what?"

I groan and laugh at once. Wes peers over, his face scrunched in a concerned frown. He mouths, "need help?"

I shake my head. "Mom, I showed you how to do that when I stopped by the house the other week. Don't you remember?"

She mutters something about not remembering, and I take another breath, prepared to spend the rest of the half-hour ride explaining to my technology-illiterate mother how to do a basic search on her computer.

Before I can speak, Wes rests his hand on my knee. "Want me to give it a try?"

I let out an exasperated sigh, then shake my head. "It's fine."

His frown turns incredulous, then he presses the speaker-phone button. "Mrs. Alexander?"

Immediately she stops chattering. "Who was that?"

"This is Wes Paulsen, your daughter's..."

When he trails off, I panic. Yes, we're living together. Yes, we've declared our feelings for each other. Yes, we openly call each other boyfriend and girlfriend. But we've never once talked about what to say about each other to our families.

"*Anak*, is this your boyfriend?"

Heat flashes up my chest to my neck, all the way to my cheeks. Somehow I'm sweating in the thirty-degree temperature.

I let out a couple of "ums" and "uhs" before Wes chuckles and says, "I am indeed your daughter's boyfriend. I'm Wes, it's nice to meet you."

The sound of Mom clapping sets echoes inside my car. "Wes, hello! So nice to talk to you! Tell me about your—"

"Mom, we're not doing this on speakerphone. We can talk about that some other time."

She huffs her disappointment.

"Mrs. Alexander, before you go, I can walk you through how to access Skype, if you still want to try."

"Oh, yes! Thank you, that would be so helpful! What a nice young man you are."

Over the next five minutes, Wes patiently walks her through it. When she finally pulls up Skype, she cheers.

"Wes, I want you to come by the house sometime," she says. "Such a kind young man, you are. Your parents must be so happy to have such a sweet and helpful son."

I squeeze his hand as he blushes. "Looking forward to it, Mrs. Alexander. Thank you."

I say goodbye before she can hammer out an exact date.

"Sorry about all that." I toss my phone in the center console.

"Don't even worry about it. Your mom sounds sweet."

"She is. Just super overbearing when it comes to her kids. Always wants to know everything we're up to. She practically freaked out when my older brother moved to Japan for his job. That means I get the bulk of her attention since we live in the same time zone, only a half-hour drive away."

I realize Wes hasn't mentioned his parents at all since we got together. "Does it bother your parents that you've been off the grid hiking the past few months? My mom would flip her lid if she couldn't get a hold of me every few days. Thank god my dad is there to calm her down."

I expect a chuckle or a reassuring anecdote about his parents, but all he gives is a murmured, "Not really."

The way he white-knuckles the steering wheel even though the road is clear makes it obvious. Family is not a subject he likes to talk about.

"It's just…" he says, his tone gentler this time.

"I didn't mean to bring up family stuff if it's a sore subject. I'm sorry."

Wes's chest heaves in a sigh. He turns his head to me and offers a sad smile. "I want you to talk about your family whenever you want. From everything you've said, they sound like wonderful people."

Eyes back on the road head, he exhales. "I'm not close with my family. At all. I don't have siblings. My mom died when I was little."

"Oh my god. I am sorry. I had no idea." I cradle his right hand in both of mine, pressing a soft kiss to his palm.

He shakes his head, pulling his hand out of my grip. He clamps it back on the wheel, his eyes straight ahead. I drop my hands to my lap, swallowing back the pain squeezing my chest. That tiny gesture, that small moment of denied contact speaks volumes. This is an off-limits topic and not even my touch makes it easier to cope.

"I lived with my dad after my mom died, but he wasn't around much."

His eyes remain glued to the road. This time when he speaks, his voice is hard. It's like a switch has flipped. Soft, sweet Wes is no longer there. The person sitting next to me in the driver's seat is a steely, closed-off version of him.

"I don't like talking about it," he says.

The stiff clench of his jaw, the way muscles in his jaw bulge against his skin illustrate that perfectly.

"Okay. I didn't mean to pry."

"It's fine." The harshness of his tone, the way he won't look at me tells me it's anything but.

I peer out my window, studying the scenery as it whizzes past. Minutes pass, all of them silent. I have no right to feel that clench in my chest, the tension in my neck, or cross my arms. Wes and I are still technically in the early days. Expecting him to deep-dive into his family issues with me is absurd.

I silently repeat this over and over in my head. But then his hand touches mine. I twist my head to look at him. There's tenderness in his face now. It helps me forget the minutes of tension that just passed between us.

He pulls the car over and turns to me. Leaning closer, he clasps my face with both of his hands. "I'm sorry for how I acted just now."

He presses a kiss to my forehead. Wrapping my hands around his wrists, I close my eyes. All the frustration and hurt feelings from minutes ago melt away, like a snowflake in a heatwave.

"The only family I have is my dad, and he's not a good person." He speaks with his mouth pressed against my forehead. Despite the sad subject, it's the most intimate, comforting feeling in the world having him speak to me like this.

"He didn't...he wasn't a good parent. He was hardly around. He never remembered my birthday. I never had a birthday party till I was in high school and my friends threw one for me."

I have to swallow to keep the lump in my throat at bay. I couldn't imagine enduring such indifference, such cruelty from my own parents. And yet Wes has dealt with it his entire life.

"When I was old enough to make my own decisions, I cut off all ties with him," he says. "My friends are my family. And you."

Another kiss on my forehead, and I melt. If I weren't sitting in the car, I'd collapse at the overwhelming joy his words give me. *Me*. I'm like family to Wes.

I lean back to look up at him. "You mean that?" I ask, my voice shaky.

"Every word."

When we kiss, my heart races. Silently, I make a promise to Wes. I don't want to ruin the peace, the closeness of this moment when he declares me his family—the family he's chosen for himself. In my head, I vow to be the family he never had, to do everything they should have done for him.

We settle back into our seats, he pulls onto the road, and I think of the most perfect surprise for him.

CHAPTER SEVEN

*T*hank goodness Wes is a summer baby. It makes it a million times easier to plan his surprise birthday party in June when the weather is warm. Trudging through the snow, ice, and slush while carrying multiple party favors is as un-fun as trips to the gynecologist or waiting in line at the DMV.

I dump two armfuls of grocery bags on the floor in the back office at Dandy Lime.

Remy peers up from the spreadsheet on his computer, eyebrow raised. "That's what you call 'just a few things?'"

"Very funny." I dump one bag, which contains streamers in every color. The remaining bags are a hodgepodge of kids' party supplies, like pin the tail on the donkey, ring toss, and stuff for sack races.

We unload the bags together. Remy holds up a container of mini candy bars and a mini bottle of rum. "What are these for?"

"The adult goodie bags I'm making."

Remy beams. "You're one hell of a thoughtful girlfriend, you know that?"

"Wes never had a birthday party as a kid."

He pats my shoulder. "He's going to love it."

"Thank you for closing the bar early tonight so we can have his birthday here."

He gives me a bear hug before digging into another shopping bag. "It's my pleasure, cuz. I owe you for all the help you've given me these past few months taking all those extra shifts."

I unspool a ream of bright blue streamer. "Always."

"It means a lot that you still help out, even though you don't need the money anymore with your business taking off."

I bite back a smile. I finished a series of watercolor landscape images inspired by that hike with Wes last month. Each one sold within a week. I've been replicating the image on smaller scale items like coasters, bags, postcards, phone cases, and magnets, which have all been a hit as well.

"No more talking about it." I scrunch my nose up at him. "I don't want to jinx anything."

"Aye aye, captain. Now, tell me exactly how you want me to decorate the place." He grabs a bag of decorations.

After decorating Remy's bar and picking up the food and cake, I've got less than two hours until Wes and I are due at the surprise party.

I throw on a yellow sundress and sandals, then swipe on makeup in the bathroom. In my head, I go over the guest list, which is me, Remy, and a dozen of Wes's friends, most of whom I remember from Valentine's Day.

I hum to myself as I remember how thrown off I felt at his friend Colin's request for a slap, the cheeky look on Wes's face, our crazy hot makeout in the women's bathroom.

The sound of Wes's keys jingling in the door snaps me out of my reminiscing session. I have to be on top of my game if I want to squeeze in everything I have planned before his surprise party.

I tie a length of red streamer across my chest, the bow resting at my cleavage. When I walk out of the bathroom door, Wes's brows jump up in shock. He scrunches up the sleeves of his crisp white dress shirt. He had meetings with clients all day, otherwise he'd be dressed in my favorite outfit of ripped jeans and a tattered, soaked-with-sweat t-shirt. But whether he's dressing for his project manager role or moonlighting as a laborer whenever a worksite is short-handed, he always looks good enough to eat.

A slow smile crawls across his face as he ruffles his thick, dark hair with a hand.

"Happy birthday, baby." I wink at him.

He walks toward me in slow, steady steps. "I thought my birthday treat was what you gave me this morning." He runs an index finger along the red bow. "I get this, too?"

I nod, then bump his nose with the tip of mine. His eyes flash.

"Pancakes and a blowjob are birthday *morning* activities," I say. "There are plenty of evening activities in store for you, too."

He doesn't bother to loosen the ribbon. He simply rips it off with one hand while the other holds my waist. My breath catches at the carnal gesture.

With his body pressed against mine, he walks me across the apartment until the backs of my knees hit the edge of the bed. I fall on my back as he drops to his knees.

"I need you," he rasps. "Now."

It's a command more than anything else. His voice is rough, his eyes are wild, and his hands are at the hem of my panties, yanking them down.

I'm panting before his mouth makes it to my skin. At this point in our relationship, just the anticipation of his mouth on me has me on the verge.

He kisses up my thighs, softly scraping his teeth along the way. I shiver and gasp at once.

"Best birthday ever," he groans.

～

"Shay, you've done enough."

Wes clutches my hand as we make our way along the sidewalk toward Dandy Lime.

I grin as we wait at the crosswalk for the light to change. "I told you, I'm taking you out to dinner tonight and that's it. I just have to stop by at Remy's to pick up my sunglasses."

It's a flimsy lie, but it's the best I could come up with after spending weeks secretly planning Wes's surprise birthday party.

Sunlight peeks from behind the skyscrapers that surround us. My heart races wondering if Wes will love or hate the kid-themed party I planned for him. When I asked what he wanted to do for his birthday weeks ago, he said all he wanted was a night spent with me. Beyond sweet, but I wanted to do something special for him.

When we round the corner to Remy's, I notice the black screen shades are drawn over the windows. Smart touch. That way Wes won't notice that there's literally no one in the bar, which would be highly unusual for seven o'clock in the evening.

When I open the door, it's dead quiet. All the lights are off, which makes it impossible to see the decorations.

"That's weird," Wes says. "It's never this dead."

Just then the lights turn on. Remy, Colin, and the rest of Wes's friends jump from behind the bar and yell, "Surprise!" in unison.

I spin to Wes, who sports wide eyes and a fallen jaw. A beat later when everyone is cheering and clapping, he beams. It's the widest, toothiest grin I've ever seen him flash. I love it more than anything.

"I can't believe…" he drifts off, his head whipping back and forth as he scans the bar.

There's a piñata hanging in one corner and pin the tail on the donkey in another. One end of the bar has been cleared for a makeshift sack race. A ping-pong table topped with red solo cups rests near the hallway by the bathrooms, ready for a game of beer pong.

He turns to me, his eyes glistening. I fight the lump in my

throat as he pulls in for a hug, his lips pressed against my forehead.

"So sneaky," he whispers.

"Sorry, I had to."

He looks down at me, still beaming. "Don't even think about apologizing. This is amazing. Thank you."

THE PLAYLIST REMY threw together hums in the background. It's the new song from EDM DJ Mari Dash. I nod along to the beat until Wes hugs me from behind, covering the side of my neck in wet kisses. I squeal and kick and laugh as he lifts me off the ground.

Already we played pin the tail on the donkey, twister, beer pong, and managed a sack race. Through it all, Wes has been smiling and laughing.

"I think you cheated at that sack race, babe." He nuzzles my neck.

I push him away, then spin around. "Such a sore loser."

He chuckles before planting yet another sloppy wet kiss on me.

"Time to redeem yourself, birthday boy." I point to the piñata. "Have at it."

He makes his way over while I head to the bar for some water.

Colin walks up and high fives me, his shaggy hair disheveled after all the falls he endured during the sack race.

"Looks like it was an easy victory for you," he says. "In a dress, no less."

I shrug and smile. "When every other competitor is pounding alcohol, it sure is."

Colin flashes a thumbs up. He's on the drunk side of tipsy, but holding up well. All of Wes's friends are, and it's one of the reasons I've grown to like them so much. All fun-loving guys who enjoy a drink, but who never let it get out of control.

Colin looks around the room. "This is really something, Shay. You did an incredible job."

I down a glass of water, then refill Colin's vodka tonic. The music from the playlist that Remy put together picks up in the background.

"Thanks again for coming, and for making sure everyone else did, too. It wouldn't have been such a great surprise if it had been just Remy and me."

Colin nods, then frowns. From the corner, Wes laughs just before Remy blindfolds him and he takes a swing at the piñata above.

"So he must have told you about it?" Colin says.

"About what?"

Colin sips his drink, then gestures around the room. He wobbles slightly, but he quickly steadies himself. "How he grew up, without all this."

"Oh. Yeah, he did."

"It's sad to even think about." He points to the games in the corner. "I was almost in tears when he finally opened up to me about all that stuff with his dad. I mean, we were best friends as kids, and I still didn't know the full story. That guy keeps his past in a vault."

I frown at him, but bite my tongue. I want to know everything about Wes's past. Maybe listening to Colin while he's tipsy and loose-lipped is my best bet at finding out more, as underhanded as it is.

"So it took a while for him to open up to you?" I ask.

He nods. "Years."

A loud burst of cheers and laughter jerks our attention back to the piñata. The rest of Wes's friends cheer him on as he lands a hit that rips open the middle of the piñata, which is in the shape of a giant letter "W." A cascade of candies falls to the floor.

"But I don't blame him," Colin says. "If my dad had been an alcoholic, I wouldn't have wanted people to know either. Never home for more than a week at a time. Poor Wes had to learn to fend for himself ever since he was five. Cooking, cleaning, laundry, homework. Pretty much everything."

I force myself to keep a neutral face as he speaks, but on the inside, I'm a million question marks. Where were his relatives when his dad was MIA? How did no one notice an elementary schooler doing all that on his own?

"Really?" My voice is soft.

"It wasn't until he moved in with my family freshman year of high school after his dad landed in prison that we all realized just how bad things were. If my parents hadn't been able to take in him, it would have been more years in foster care for him."

"Foster care?"

In the background, another EDM song plays, but I don't even hear it. My thoughts are focused on what Colin just revealed. Wes was in foster care as a kid?

Tipsy Colin continues. "He already spent most of middle school being bounced around from stranger's home to stranger's home. He didn't deserve to go through that for another four years when his dad got locked up for good."

I say nothing, letting the long pause stretch between us. Invisible blocks fall into place in my mind as I scramble to put things together. Wes's dad went to prison and as a result, he fell into the foster care system. Now it makes sense why he never talks about him or the things he did as a kid. It also makes sense why he and Colin are so close. I didn't know they shared a home in high school.

My stomach churns as I stay silent, waiting for Colin to take another sip and say more. It's not right the way I time my pauses, knowing that if I wait long enough, Colin will keep spilling even more about Wes's past—the past Wes has only shared tidbits of. But I have to know more.

Colin drunkenly grooves along to the song. "Damn, I love Mari Dash." He knocks back the rest of his drink and pats me on the shoulder. "Pee break."

He heads to the back of the bar toward the restroom, while I grip a nearby table to steady myself. This peek into Wes's past has shocked me to the core.

This man that I live with, this man that I fall for more and more every day, doesn't feel comfortable sharing his past with me. And it kills.

～

I TUMBLE into the shower the second we arrive home at my apartment. Under the stream of hot water, I close my eyes. The rational part of my brain knows that I have no right to expect Wes to tell me anything about his past. He's been nothing but honest and upfront since the moment we've met. He's never lied, never cheated, never deceived. He's not under any obligation to spill everything about his childhood to me.

But that's what you do when you grow close to someone, when you're in a relationship. Most people want to open up to their partners because it's a sign they care about them deeply.

I'm an open book when I'm with Wes. I've told him about my family, my past. He listens with genuine interest, always asking me questions, always wanting to know more.

When I'm with Wes, I *want* to tell him everything. But I want him to feel that same way about me. And right now, it's clear he doesn't.

It's a sign. I don't make him feel safe or secure, like how he makes me feel.

"Shay, you good?"

Wes's voice cuts through my thoughts. I cough past the tightness in my throat. "Fine."

A whoosh of cold air hits my back when the shower curtain

parts behind me. The heat from Wes's naked body as he stands behind me is an instant comfort, despite the doubt tucked away inside of me.

When his hands slide around my waist, my muscles give and I practically fall into him. He nuzzles his face into the side of my neck. Goosebumps flash across my skin, despite the fact that the hot water from the shower has turned this tiny space into a mini steam room.

"Baby," he whispers. "Thank you so much for tonight. It's the most thoughtful thing anyone has done for me."

I swallow back the questions I have no right to ask. Instead, I breathe. "I'm so glad."

Palms on my hips, he turns me to face him. He stares, his eyes displaying the trademark intensity that always makes them shine so bright.

He blinks, then presses his forehead against mine. "I'm lucky Colin ran up to me after I hugged you when we first walked in. I would have lost it otherwise."

Water droplets cover his body. Under the harsh bathroom lighting, they shine like a million tiny gems. I have to swallow back a gasp. He looks so raw, so full of emotion, so damn beautiful.

When he smiles, his eyes glisten. It's a second before I realize he's holding back tears. He's opening up. It's slow—slower than I would like, but it still means everything. It shows just how strongly he feels for me, just how much I must mean to him.

Slowly, I slide my hands from his chest to his face. I take my time, savoring each inch of flesh under my touch. I want to remember everything about this moment. The look in his eyes, the way he holds me against him, the emotion coursing through him that's so powerful, I could swear I feel it in me, too.

"I'm so lucky you're mine." His voice shakes when he says it.

There's no time to comment though because soon his mouth is on mine. Under a sheet of steam and water, our tongues tease and collide. The kisses between us are wet fire, igniting us from the inside, exploding in invisible flames around us.

Every lick, every taste of him in my mouth is pure heat, just like every other kiss we've shared. This time is different for me, though. Wes doesn't say it, but I know it is for him, too. Everything about the way he gazes at me, the words he spoke to me just now, the way he's grabbing at my body like he never, ever wants to let go, sends the message loud and clear.

Wes is letting me in.

Wet, warm hands hold my face, tilting me up to look at him. I'm locked into that burnt umber stare, hypnotized forever.

"You are everything to me, Shay." He speaks through broken breath, water dripping from his face, his eyes still fire. "You know that, right?"

I nod. Even though I know he's still holding back, I know he means this. And it's enough for me right now.

"You know that you're everything to me too, don't you?" I gasp.

I hope he hears the conviction in my voice; I hope he knows that since he's my everything, he can tell me everything too.

There's a nod from and another desperate string of kisses. One of his hands slides down between my legs. His thick fingers press against me, and the heat is like heaven. He moves in quick circles, each one twisting me tighter and tighter into myself.

He scrapes his teeth against my shoulder, and I groan. Tilting his head, he leans his mouth to my ear. "You have me, Shay. Every last part of me."

His growl shoves me right to the edge. Another few circles and I'm gone, freefalling off the edge.

I scream *yes*, I scream *please*, I scream *more*. He delivers, sliding his fingers inside me as I ride out the rest of my orgasm on wobbly knees. If his hands are soft bliss, his body is a concrete haven. I thrash and grab and bite him through my climax, but he stays as still.

When I come down, I grab the back of his neck with one hand. The other slides from his shoulder to the hardness between his legs.

I kiss and lick over the claw marks I left on his shoulder, but all he does is smile. "Hottest thing in the world is seeing your marks on me."

With him in my palm, I slide back and forth. His smile turns to a straight line of concentration a minute later. I dollop body wash into my hand and quicken my strokes. He responds with a growl and eyebrows pinched together.

That far-off stare takes over his eyes. I tip-toe up to kiss him.

"You have me too, Wes," I say into his mouth after another kiss. "All of me."

Burying his face into my shoulder, he presses his teeth against my skin. The perfect balance of pleasure and pain. He spills into my hand seconds later.

While he breathes through his own comedown, I wrap my hands around him, pressing soft kisses across his chest. My own chest swells with joy, with an emotional satisfaction I've never known before. In this moment, it's all okay. Maybe Wes can't speak the words that I want him to say right now, but his body has told me so much more. And it's enough. If I can have him like this —his feelings, his stare, his heart all mine—I can wait for the words.

CHAPTER EIGHT

"*T*hanks again for agreeing to come." I gaze over at Wes sitting in the passenger seat of my car.

The smile he flashes is tight. I don't blame him at all. Meeting the parents is never fun. I've done it a few times myself with guys I've dated and it's always nerve-racking. Best case scenario, it's awkward hugging and stilted conversation. Worst case scenario, it's so uncomfortable you wish you could peel your skin off just to have something else to do.

I was careful when I asked him if he wanted to meet them yesterday. Mom had been bombarding me with texts and calls over the past week, asking when I was finally going to bring my new boyfriend over for her and Dad to meet. Finally, I gave in and asked Wes if he'd be up for it. With that same tight smile on his face, he said yes.

With one hand on the steering wheel, I reach for his hand. The gentle squeeze I give him seems to do something. He turns his stare from the road ahead to me. His eyes thaw to something more tender; his brow smooths from its wrinkled frown.

"Seriously, thank you," I say. "It really does mean a lot that you're meeting them. Gushing about you over the phone just isn't cutting it anymore."

My try for something lighthearted to ease his nerves seems to have worked. The soft laugh he lets out is music to my ears after a twenty-minute silence during this car ride.

"That's a lot to live up to," he says, his lightly tanned cheeks flushing red.

"Just be yourself. You'll blow them away."

When I pull into my parents' block, I scan the dozen cars lining the street. One of their neighbors must be having a get-together. I pull into their driveway, then take Wes's hand in mine as we walk up to the door.

Before I can offer a few last words of encouragement, Mom bursts out the front door, arms as wide as her smile as she trots to us.

She pays me a brief moment of eye contact before pulling Wes down into a hug. Even with him bent at the waist to meet her tiny size, he still dwarfs her five-foot-tall self.

"It's so nice to finally meet you!" she says in her signature sing-song voice. With Wes in her embrace, she sways back and forth, like she's rocking a baby.

Wes twists his head, his wide, unblinking gaze meeting mine. Again I open my mouth to say sorry and politely tell her to release him from her death-hug, but then my dad trots out from the front door.

"Oh, Gloria. Let the poor guy go before you crack his ribs." He pats his slight potbelly before chuckling. He pulls me into a hug before I can do anything to help Wes. "How you doin', sweetie? Good to see you."

"Thanks, Dad." My voice comes out muffled against his shoulder. He clears six feet, so even his side hugs engulf me.

He releases me at the same moment Mom finally lets Wes out of her hold. I bend down to hug her, mouthing "sorry" to Wes. A hesitant smile appears. "It's okay," he mouths back.

I let out a sigh of sweet relief when Dad offers him a friendly handshake and not a bear hug.

"Come inside!" Mom says, waving us in. "Everyone is so excited to see you both!"

My stomach and heart fall in tandem to my feet when I step inside. Instead of the quiet lunch with just my parents that I promised Wes, my entire extended family who lives in the area is crammed into their home.

Wes and I are rushed by a wave of cousins and aunties and uncles. Instantly, we're pulled into hugs and given cheek kisses. Laughter and excited questions echo around us. It's sensory overload, but I'm used to it—this is how every family gathering goes. But Wes isn't. All he had growing up were his friends and his dad, who was never around. Judging from what Colin said, Wes has never experienced a large gathering of relatives trying to smother him with affection.

That's why even though on the outside I'm sputtering pleasantries, I'm discreetly scanning the room for Wes. This must be a nightmare for him, all these strangers itching to hug him.

I quickly answer a question from my cousin about my art website before my gaze lands on Wes, who is now on the other side of the living room having his cheeks pinched by my Great Aunt Nima. When she starts to ask him about marriage and kids, I make a beeline for them. Poor Wes doesn't need to be put on the spot by auntie Nima when the two of us haven't even had that conversation.

But then Mom catches my elbow, halting me. "Honey! What a sweetheart Wes is! Look how well he's taking to the family!"

She points over at him still standing with Auntie Nima. She releases him, but judging by the tense smile on his face and how he stands with his arms crossed, he isn't comfortable at all.

I turn to her. "Why did you invite the whole family over? This was supposed to be just lunch with you and Dad."

She waves her hand in the air. "I thought this would be so

much more fun. And almost everyone could make it. Well, except Remy because he had to work, but he's met Wes before, so it's fine. It's been so long since we've done a big family gathering. Wasn't it a nice surprise?"

I sigh, silently ordering myself to rein in my frustration. I can't lash out at her, not in front of everyone. She did this with the best of intentions. That doesn't erase the anxiety so obviously coursing through Wes though. What I would give for Remy to be here. At least he would have been a familiar face in the crowd.

"It's just all a bit overwhelming for Wes," I say.

She frowns and shakes her head. "Don't be ridiculous. Look. He's fine."

For a split second, I contemplate telling her that his stand-offish posture and pursed lips are the exact opposite of fine, but she walks away to talk to my uncle before I can get a word in.

I look up in Wes's direction, but he's disappeared. My heart pounds. In the time that I stopped and talked to my mom, I'm sure at least one other relative has asked him the marriage and kids question. Or maybe one of my cousins has dragged him off for that dreaded topic of "just what are your intentions with our Shay?"

I spin around and catch him out of the corner of my eye nodding as my uncle is showing him photos from his wallet. I move to head over, but one of my cousin's kids stops me to help get her a snack. When I finish helping her and look for Wes, he's gone again. I sigh and trudge through the crowd once more.

"I'm so, so sorry about that, Wes." I focus on the road ahead, bracing myself for his response.

It was a solid forty-five minutes before I could find Wes in the crowd of my family. He was in the den listening to my great uncle complain about social security benefits. By the dazed look on his face, he had had enough. I snatched him and we left soon after that when I made up an excuse that I wasn't feeling well.

Seconds pass, but Wes says nothing. I peer over at him in the passenger seat of my car. I nearly jolt at the stony look in his eyes, the hard line of his mouth. But part of me expects this. He's not used to family, to huge, loud, touchy-feely gatherings that go on for hours. Shutting down is a normal response when a person is overwhelmed. I know this. And I want to help him through it.

"My mom does that sometimes, invites the whole family over when it's supposed to be a small gathering," I try to explain. "I've had my whole life to get used to it, but still it gets on my nerves."

There's no answer. He won't even look at me.

The drive finishes in strained silence. We walk up the stairs to my apartment that same way. When I lock the door behind me, I turn to him, wondering how to gently approach him in a way that encourages him to open up to me so I can help him through whatever he's feeling.

He chucks his wallet and keys on the table in the corner before spinning around to me. His frown is back, but this time with an edge. He rests his hands on his hips before he finally speaks. "Why didn't you tell me your entire family might be there today?"

"I didn't know they would be. My mom sprung it on us as a surprise."

"But you said she does this sometimes." His jaw clenches. "Why didn't you say that earlier?"

I open my mouth, but can't think of anything to say. I probably should have thought to do that. It just never crossed my mind.

When I say nothing, he turns away, shaking his head.

"I know it was kind of shocking what she did, but she meant well," I finally say. "She was just excited about meeting you. Sometimes she gets carried away like that. But you handled it so well."

When I step toward him, he holds a hand up. His frown turns lethal. I halt like I've been shoved away.

"Kind of shocking?" Wes's tone amps up a notch. And it's so

69

hard, so brutal that my ears ring. "You think today was just 'kind of shocking?' That's hilarious."

He turns to the bed, kicking his backpack out from the corner. I follow him and rest my hand on his shoulder, but a half-second later he shrugs out of my touch.

"Don't," he barks.

I pull away like I've just singed my fingers on a hot stove. That's the only move I can make at the moment. The rest of my body is frozen still at the anger in his voice, the way his body just rejected mine.

He spins around to face me. "Do you have any idea what it's like to be thrown into that kind of setting with no warning at all?"

I don't answer because I don't have the slightest clue what to say. Because he's right. I don't know the first thing about what life has been like for him.

"I didn't grow up like you, Shay. I didn't have a happy family or a happy home life like you. I was a kid whose own dad couldn't take care of me."

He speaks to the floor, not me. It's a weird kind of detachment that makes my chest ache.

"And then I had your entire family bombard me with questions about when we're getting married and having kids? Shit, *we* haven't even talked about that."

I cringe thinking about how awful that must have felt for him to endure those questions without me there to buffer them.

He keeps a normal volume, but it's the way the words jump from his tongue, harsh and unrelenting, as if they're poison. And it's all for me.

He crouches on the floor next to his backpack and unzips it. I walk over and crouch across from him.

"I'm sorry they did that, but it's not like I put them up to it," I say, my voice strained. "It's just normal family stuff that happens when someone brings home their significant other. I get that you're upset, but please don't be angry with me about this."

I pause, waiting for him to say something, anything. But he doesn't. My skin pricks once more at how dismissive he's being.

My head spins. "Wes, how was I supposed to anticipate all this when you never told me that this sort of thing would upset you? I had to find out what happened to you from Colin," I blurt.

Wes's frown turns to pure shock. He stands to his feet slowly. I follow.

"You found out what from Colin?"

The new softness in his tone doesn't erase any of the anger. It actually cuts deeper. I've only ever heard that low, soft growl when he's hugged me from behind and whispered all the naughty things he plans to do to me. That soft tone used to make me melt. Now it makes my skin crawl. What an absolute mindfuck.

I swallow, matching my volume with his. "How after your dad went to jail, you went into foster care. How you eventually moved in with Colin's family." My throat squeezes.

One look from Wes and all my anger morphs to pain. I can tell by the flush on his cheeks, how he refuses to meet my eyes, he hates that I know all this about him. And that's what hurts the most. I'm the one person in the world he should feel comfortable telling anything to, and yet he still wants to hide.

"You knew? This whole time?"

"I found out on your birthday. Colin was drunk and told me. I'm so sorry." Again I reach for him, but he pulls away.

He turns his back to me once more. "I'm not a charity case, Shay."

"No, that's not what I…that's not why…"

My words fall off a cliff as soon as I see him open up the two drawers of my dresser that I set aside for him. He shoves handfuls of his clothes into his duffle bag on the floor. Then he darts around me to the tiny wall closet. The sound of metal hangers clanking against wood fills our stilted silence. I watch as he emerges with his suitcase and tosses the rest of his clothes and shoes inside.

"Wes, what are you doing?"

It's a pointless question because I already know the answer. I watch in a daze, as if my body is trapped in a time warp with everything around me happening in real-time. All I can do is stand off to the side like a statue and stare.

It's not until he zips up his bags and turns to face me that I snap back to life.

"Wait." It comes out more like a gasp than a word. When I blink, tears tumble down my cheeks. I grab him by the wrists and pull him to me. "I know your life was hard growing up, but you don't have anything to be ashamed about. It made you who you are today, and I love you. Every single thing about you, I love. Yeah, this is rough, but we can make this—us—work."

Wes's stony expression flinches when I say the word "love." But it's true. Even though I wish I could have said it in a different setting, when we're not hurt and angry and on the verge of collapsing, I mean it. I've never fallen for anyone this fast, this hard before. I love Wes, and I want to mend this rift between us. I want to make everything better. All I want is him.

A beat later Wes's beautiful face is hard again. For endless seconds I wait for the words, for him to tell me he loves me too, that he'll stay so we can work things out. But all I get is my name on his lips. It's cold, unfeeling. My chest cracks in half. I never thought that Wes speaking my name could break me.

"Shay," he repeats. It's hard, unrelenting, and not at all like the man I know. "I can't do this anymore."

"What?" My voice is strangled, I'm so shocked by his reply.

"Marriage, family, kids, huge surprise gatherings with relatives."

"Wes, I'm not asking you to marry me or have kids or—"

"But you want all that. Eventually. Right?"

I stay silent, stunned at how he's using this as a reason to leave me. I open my mouth to object, but I can't. Because Wes is right. I want all of those things. What happened today with my family was an annoying surprise, but it's part of my life. Deep down, I couldn't imagine not having kids one day, my own family to bring to one of my mom's giant surprise gatherings.

His frown deepens the longer he looks at me. "I know we never talked about it, but...look, I thought I could get on board with family and kids someday, but after today, I don't think I'll be able to handle any of that."

"You could handle Colin's family," I finally say. It's such a pathetic argument to make, but it's all I can come up with to try to get him to reconsider.

"That was different." He sighs, almost like he's annoyed that I've brought that up. "It was just him, his parents, and me. And I knew them for years."

Loaded silence takes over once more as I process what he's saying.

"You want everything I don't, Shay," he says. "Tell me I'm wrong."

I won't lie, but I can't bring myself to say the words. So I stay quiet.

"This is too much. I can't handle it. I'm meant to be on my own. And you belong with someone who wants what you want." He stops speaking as his voice starts to break.

When he walks toward the door, I'm right behind him. When he reaches for the doorknob, I reach for his hand. This time, when I turn him to me, when I hold his face in my hands, when I press the front of my body against the front of his, he doesn't move away, he doesn't flinch. He doesn't reject me.

I will myself to stand against him, still as stone. We could stay like this forever. I would do it if it meant that I could keep him with me.

"I love you, Wes. Please stay. Please give us a chance." I pause to steady my voice despite my urge to sob.

Snot and tears cover my face, which I'm sure is as red as the paint on my canvas. I am every shade of pathetic, there's no doubt. But his frown, his unfeeling stare says it all.

"I can't. I'm sorry, Shay."

One step back and one turn around are all it takes for him to escape me. When the door shuts, he's gone.

I don't run after him. I stand, silent sobs shaking my body, the knowledge of how little I meant to Wes as clear as the sunlight shining through my window.

I don't even collapse from the sadness. Instead, I stay standing, right where he left me, a statue once more.

CHAPTER NINE

*T*he two empty tequila bottles on my coffee table say it all.

One week since Wes and I broke up, and I'm a disaster. Dirty laundry and dishes scatter my apartment. I haven't bothered to make my bed in days. I can't remember the last time I showered. For seven straight days, all I can remember doing is alternating between sitting on my couch and sleeping on it, with long stretches of guzzling tequila whenever I thought the pain in my chest was going to kill me.

I sit up and stare out the only window in my studio apartment. It's sunny, but I have no idea if that means it's morning or afternoon. My phone died yesterday and I haven't bothered to charge it.

I glance at my phone, still dead on the coffee table. It's not like it would make a difference if my phone was even working. Not once has Wes called or texted since leaving. The only way I even know that he's alive is because I texted Colin a few days ago asking if he had heard from him. Because texting your ex's friend after he breaks up with you is only a tiny bit less pathetic than texting your ex.

But that got me nothing other than an apologetic message from Colin saying that he didn't know where Wes was headed, just that he was gone.

I wish I had more to tell you, but I don't. He turned in his notice a few days ago and didn't tell me where he'd be heading.

The fact that Wes iced out his best friend blew me away. But then the second text Colin completely annihilated me.

You two were great together. I honestly don't know what got into him. I've never seen him like this.

I tear up for the millionth time when I remember the hopelessness that overtook me when I read it. If his own best friend has no hope, I shouldn't either.

Wes isn't ever coming back.

I contemplate a run to the convenience store for another bottle of tequila when there's pounding at my front door.

"Shay! You alive?"

I recognize Remy's panicked boom right away. I shoot up from the couch, then hunch over when a dizzy spell hits. Eating minimal food while binge-drinking hard liquor these past several days has turned me into a walking hangover. I don't exist in any sort of worthwhile form anymore. I can't ignore Remy, though. Judging by how he keeps pounding at the door, he'll break it down rather than leave me in peace.

When I get my balance back, I wobble to the door and open it.

"Thank god." He pulls me into a hug, then immediately pulls away, his brown eyes wide. Then he cups a hand over his face. "What the hell happened to you? And why the hell do you smell like a dumpster?"

I wave a hand at him, then collapse back onto the couch. His heavy footsteps trail behind me. A second later he's standing in front of me, only the coffee table separating us.

He leers over me, pointing at the empty glass bottles. "What is that? Why the hell haven't you answered any of my calls or texts this past week?"

"Say 'hell' again. That'll make me answer faster."

His chest rises in a single frustrated breath. "Do you have any idea how worried your mom is? She called me yesterday and the day before asking about you because you wouldn't answer your phone. Why are you ignoring her? You know the moms and aunties in our family go berserk when they can't get ahold of their kids for more than a day."

I shrug, trying to play it off like I don't have a pounding headache that's about to split my head in two. "I've been busy."

"Busy drinking yourself to death and refusing to bathe?"

He swipes up both bottles and tosses them in the trashcan just a few feet away. Then he resumes the position of standing over me, irritation plastered across his face. "Explain. Now."

"I was feeling down. That's all."

Arms crossed over his broad chest, he leans over me. "I thought you were dead or kidnapped. You need to explain to me what happened that turned you into such a sad sack."

As annoyed as I am, I can't blame him. If he or my brother went missing for days, I'd be worried sick too. But once he figures out the reason for my self-imposed hermit status is because of a breakup, he's going to freak. What a pitiful reason to completely let myself go.

Tears blur my vision. I blink and look up at the dark blob hovering over me that I assume is Remy. "Wes broke up with me."

Remy plops next to me on the couch and cradles me while I sob out the entire story. I tell him how Wes meeting my parents turned into a colossal mistake when Mom decided to invite our entire extended family as a surprise. And then I give him a quick summary of Wes's past and how it played into everything.

"Good god," Remy mutters, hugging me tightly.

"He hasn't even bothered to contact me since he left," I sob. "No call, no text. Nothing."

Remy's giant paws grip me by the shoulders. He turns me to face him head-on. "Look, I'm mad as hell that Wes broke up with you. But I'll be damned if I'm going to sit here and watch you waste away over him. You've had a week to be sad. Enough wallowing. Time to function like a human being again."

My mouth trembles with the urge to sob once more. "I...I don't know if I can."

"Cuz, *I* know you can. And you will. You're my feisty, confident cousin who can handle anything—annoying douchebros at my bar, a scary career change, and everything else in between. Look, breakups suck. I know that more than anyone. But you can't let them destroy you. You have to move on."

"But what if I don't know how?"

Remy winks at me. "Fake it till you make it."

I sob at chuckle at the same time. It's the first happy-like sound I've made in days.

He wraps his arm around me once more, and I settle against his barrel chest. "Aww, cuz, did I make you laugh? After a full week of crying and drinking? I'd say I deserve a trophy for that."

This time, a string of proper chuckles falls from me.

"Well, that one sounded a bit snotty, but I'll take it."

I breathe. "I've gone through breakups before, Remy. This one hit hard though..."

I stop myself before I say the "L" word.

"That's because you love him. Love makes everything better—and worse. The pain of losing someone you love is unbearable."

I glance up at him, wiping my nose on the sleeve of my hoodie. "How do you get through it?"

"Baby steps. One day at a time."

"Are you just going to parrot self-help phrases at me now?"

"You're getting your feistiness back. That's promising." He laughs. "How about helping me at the bar tonight?"

I groan. "Remy, I don't know if I have it in me to deal with other human beings right now."

"Just try it. If after an hour you can't stand it, you can go home.

But you need to make yourself do normal, everyday things, even if it hurts. It's the best way to feel like yourself again."

He's right. When I stop thinking about Wes, there's a sudden burst of hope. It hits right at the center of my chest, cutting through the pain. It's tiny and fleeting, but it's there. For the first time in days, I don't feel like collapsing and sobbing on the floor. I don't feel good—not by a long shot—but with Remy's help, I feel better. I feel human again. And that's something.

"We'll even do a shot of tequila to kick things off if you want," he says.

I glare at him, shaking my head. "No. No more tequila. Ever."

Remy shoots a confused frown at me. "Excuse me, but I'm the one who turned you on to the good stuff. I gave you that decent stuff when you started your website—"

I hold up my hand. "Tequila was mine and Wes's drink."

This time when he glances at the empty tequila bottles scattering my living room, a look of recognition flashes across his face. I have to move on now, just like Remy said. That means not touching tequila for the foreseeable future.

I sniffle. "If I have any hope of getting over him, I can't…"

Remy nods once. "Enough said." He gives me a light tap on my back. "Now get yourself in that shower and scrub like you've never scrubbed before."

CHAPTER TEN

I tuck an order form in the envelope and seal it, then check the clock. "Damn it."

The post office is closing in twenty minutes. I'll never make it.

The momentary frustration melts away and all I feel is exhaustion—but for the best possible reason. My business is picking up. Every day I'm painting, sketching, creating.

One month post-breakup, and I'm surviving. I catch my reflection in the window and run my fingers through my newly short hair. This shoulder-length bob has been difficult to get used to, but it was a needed change. I needed to shed the long hair that Wes loved so much. Every time I brushed it, braided it, ran my fingers through it, I ached. So I said goodbye to thirteen inches and donated it. Through the reflection, I give myself a soft smile. I have to admit that I wear this new style well.

That first night back at Dandy Lime wasn't easy, but Remy was right. It was necessary. It showed me I could go through the motions of daily life even through the pain. And that's what I do, night after night, day after day. I shower, get dressed, put on makeup, eat, and work during the day. At night, I run the bar with

Remy. I'm so exhausted by the end of the evening that I don't have time to wallow.

I'm not completely out of the woods, though. Every week it gets easier, but it's not without its dark moments. Last week a guy walked into Dandy Lime wearing the exact same red and black flannel shirt Wes wore the night we met, and I froze. I should have suspected it. It's September—autumn—and that means everyone will be wearing flannel. But all I could do was stare at the stranger, then excuse myself to the back room where I had to calm myself with deep breaths and a hushed pep talk.

It's okay. I'll be okay. Just breathe.

Crazy how a random piece of fabric has the ability to destroy weeks of progress. But I deep-breathed my way through the setback and worked the rest of the night.

I am fine. I *will* be fine.

My phone beeps with a text from my mom.

Mom: *Anak. You okay? You need more food?*

Ever since I came clean to mom about the breakup with Wes, she's been fussing over me. Multiple phone calls and texts every day to check in, in addition to a handful of surprise food deliveries. Even my dad, who showered me with loads of concerned calls the week after I told them about my breakup, tells her to ease up on me daily.

I let out a sigh, reminding myself that she's fussing because she loves me.

Me: *I'm doing fine, mom. I still have that container of fried rice and the pansit you dropped off the other day.*

Mom: *Okay, that's good! I love you! Don't forget to eat! And call or text me anytime you need anything!*

I text "I love you" to her, then stop to eat leftovers. When I sit back at my desk, my phone beeps again. An alert from Instagram.

I squint at the heavily filtered photo of a woman clad in a white one-piece bathing suit facing a window in a chicly decorated living room. Only her back is visible. When I tap the photo, my Instagram handle pops up. And that's when I see it.

One of my watercolor cityscapes is framed on the white wall of her living room. I smile to myself, giddy that someone likes my art enough to post about it on social media.

I skim the caption below the photo.

Finally finished decorating my new flat. Absolutely LOVE this piece by artist @ShayAlexander. My #cali home feels complete now #californiadreamin #lifeloveart #artfanatic #shayfanatic

When I focus on the name of the account, I almost choke on a swallow. Mari Dash, the famous DJ, is the woman in the photo. She has a million followers and just tagged me in her post.

I choke for real when I see that her photo boasts a few thousand likes and comments.

That painting is almost as gorgeous as you are, Mari!

OMG who is this @ShayAlexander person?? I need her artwork ASAP!

I heave a breath. Tickets to her concerts sell out in minutes. How in the world did she stumble upon my tiny, insignificant website? She could probably afford a Picasso for crying out loud.

I shove the thought to the back of my brain. How she found me doesn't matter. What matters is that a celebrity is a fan of my artwork and that means a level of exposure I've never had before.

I indulge in a few seconds of jumping up and down and squealing. And then I check my email inbox.

Holy fucking shit.

Fifty-seven new orders for various pieces of my artwork have just filtered through my site. With unblinking, disbelieving eyes, I quickly scan the orders for digital prints I've designed, my canvas paintings, sketches, pretty much everything I sell on my site.

I grip the back of my desk chair to steady myself. I try and fail to stand up straight.

"Oh my god."

I think I just got my big break.

I check the clock. An hour until I'm due at Dandy Lime for my shift.

Shock turns to laser focus. I call Remy. Holding the phone between my chin and my shoulder, I plop down at my desk and start working on the orders. My smile is so wide that my cheeks ache, but I don't care.

Remy answers on the third ring.

I pause for a beat to inhale. "Guess what just happened?"

"What? Is everything okay?"

"More than okay. Try freaking fantastic."

"What is it?" Remy's voice goes pitchy and breathy, a sign I've sold this well.

"You know that DJ Mari Dash?"

"Of course. I love her."

"She bought one of my paintings and tagged me in her Instagram post. The orders are pouring in." I click my mouse like a madwoman. "I don't want to jinx things, but I think this could be big. I got fifty-seven orders on my website just from her post being up for half an hour."

"Oh my god, cuz!"

"You took the words right out of my mouth."

A MONTH after I blew up on social media and I'm still riding the wave. I'm spending my daylight hours painting and sketching, then the evenings processing orders from my website and updating social media.

Already I'm reaping the benefit. I'm earning more money than I ever have. I peek around from behind my easel out the window.

"Holy crap," I mutter when I take in the dark sky. I could have sworn that just minutes ago, it was daylight.

I pad to the kitchen and pull out a carton of eggs. Scrambled eggs and toast are a sorry substitute for dinner, but I don't want to do anything other than work. The big break I've been waiting years for finally happened. I'll do everything I can to make it last.

When I finish eating, I contemplate a shower, but as I gaze out the window, I'm taken by the cityscape glittering in the distance. It would make one hell of an oil pastel rendering in my brand-new sketchbook.

I open the drawer of my desk, lift up the sketchbook, then freeze at the sight of what's underneath.

Wes's face. Wes's beautiful, flawless, perfectly angular face stares back at me in black and white. It's a charcoal rendering of him, my favorite one that I've ever drawn. I lift the corner of the sheet up to reveal his perfect face once more, this time in water-color. My favorite painting of him and my favorite sketch of him, hidden away all this time.

The evening when Wes and I made things official replay in my mind like a highlight reel. I swallow, but the inside of my mouth and throat are so dry, I end up coughing. So, so foolish.

It's the stranger in the red and black flannel moment from last month, but with a dagger to the heart added in for good measure. I wasn't ready to see Wes's face this close, this clear.

These are paintings, images—nowhere close to the real thing, but they still look exactly like him. The only thing worse would be him in the flesh right next to me. And if I want to continue moving on, I have to get rid of everything Wes around me.

I pull out my camera, place the artwork on the floor, adjust the lighting, and take photos. Then I upload them to my website along with information about dimensions. The blank spaces for the title of the works stare back at me, burning my eyes. It's never been this hard to title my own work.

But this time is different—it's personal in the worst possible way. So personal is what I go with.

Wes, watercolor
Wes, black and white

The truth and nothing more.

I grab two large envelopes from my stash and shove the drawings inside of them. Judging by how quickly my other work has been selling, these two will go quickly. But I don't want to accidentally catch glimpses of them in the meantime.

I stack the envelopes in an empty box and sit at my desk once more. With my heartbeat and breath finally steady, I pick up a pencil and my new pad. Just the graphite tip hitting paper focuses my mind. The texture, the soft sound, the blank space filling with lines. Such a simple movement, but it gives me so much. It centers me and cleanses me all at once.

And right now, at this moment, I need that more than anything.

IF I HAD Mari Dash's phone number, I'd call her so I could tell her thank you over and over. Because of her, I'm spending twelve hours a day painting, sketching, filling orders, mailing orders, designing and selling prints, taking on more commissions than I ever thought I would—and I couldn't be happier.

Every day since she posted my painting on her Instagram account two months ago, my phone has been dinging nonstop with alerts. It sounds every time someone on Twitter or Instagram tags me in a photo with whatever art piece of mine they've just purchased. Other famous influencers that are connected with Mari online have been buying my work and posting photos online, which has cascaded into even more sales.

I move from the cross-legged sitting position on the floor and sprawl flat on my back to stretch. I should go for a run or do some yoga on the floor right now, but I'm not even close to interested. I scan the floor, smiling at the pile of cardboard boxes and packing materials that surround me. Around my make-shift studio space lies a dozen canvases swathed in paint or charcoal, drying before I pack them up and mail them.

I've been up since six this morning; it's currently just past noon, and this is the first break I've taken. I'm sore, exhausted, sleep-deprived, and deliriously happy. Because finally, my dream is coming true. I'm a full-time artist who can pay my bills with just the income from my artwork.

My phone blaring yanks me out of my bliss bubble. I crawl to my phone, which sits on my desk chair and answer.

"Hi, is this Shay Alexander?" A female voice says.

"Yes, this is Shay. Who's calling?" I reach for the glass of water on my desk to sip while answering the call.

"This is Mari Dash."

I promptly spit up the water I was sipping, then spend a good thirty seconds hacking up one of my lungs.

"Are you okay?" Mari asks in her trademark sing-song voice.

Automatically I nod, but then remember she can't see me. I clear my throat. "Y-yeah. Sorry...uh, down the wrong pipe."

"Oh, I hate when that happens." She chuckles. "So! I know this is last minute, but I figured that Bend is only a few hours from Portland and it never hurts to ask. Are you free this Saturday night? I'm performing at Portis, this new club on Glisan Street, and I want you to come."

This time when I choke, it's on the air I'm swallowing. It's a struggle just to process the words coming from her mouth. Mari Dash is personally inviting me to her concert? How the hell did she even get my phone number?

Another few seconds of coughing commences until I'm able to speak again. When I do, it's to ask her the second question I'm wondering.

"Your website." She laughs. And then I remember that I listed my phone number on it when I first designed it—it's just that most people these days would prefer to interact online instead of calling.

Except for Mari, apparently.

"You're such an inspiring artist—your artwork inspired me to change the entire aesthetic of my home decor. And I would love to meet you in person."

I bite my bottom lip as I struggle to process the fact that Mari Dash wants to meet me.

"Please say you're free! I want you to sign the prints of yours I just ordered too!"

I take a breath, heart racing, my own smile threatening to split my face in half. "I'd love to."

CHAPTER ELEVEN

*S*tanding at the far edge of the stage at the Portis venue, I do another slow scan of the scene around me. I can see everything perfectly from here. I can see Mari as she grooves from behind her turntable, jumping up and down to the thudding beat of her EDM song. I can see the crowd as they jump in unison with her. I can see the light tech all the way at the top balcony on the opposite side of the venue. The exposed brick walls and industrial ceiling beams give the venue a stripped-down look that's perfect for this kind of concert. As people sing and dance along to her music, it's clear they don't care about anything other than being in Mari's presence.

Even though it's a chilly and rainy Saturday evening in Portland, it's all heat in here. The sheer number of bodies combined with the near-constant jumping has upped the temperature inside the venue to at least twenty degrees warmer than outside.

But even as sweat beads across my skin, I can't help but smile and sway along to the beat. This night has been a life highlight for me. As soon as I arrived at Portis and gave my name to the security guy standing in front of the door, I was ushered inside and down a long hallway to a closed door at the end. When the door opened, there was Mari Dash, standing in a glittery white body-suit and black leather stiletto boots that ran all the way to the middle of her thighs. Her jet-black hair was pulled into a loose chignon. Even though she was standing right in front of me, she looked too perfect to be human.

I suddenly felt unglamorous in the flowy top, dark skinny leggings, and boots I was sporting.

But before I could stutter a "hello," she pulled me into a hug. "You're here! Finally!"

She popped a bottle of champagne before shooing the security guy away and shutting the door to her dressing room. She poured two glasses, handed me one, then gestured for me to take a seat on one end of the plush couch.

"So!" She plopped on the other end. "How do you feel about signing some swag for me?" She pointed to a stack of portrait-sized prints on her vanity. "I'm giving them as gifts for people for Christmas. Can you believe it's almost December? This year is just flying by."

Speechless, I nodded. Sitting on Mari's vanity was three months' worth of income for me.

She leaned over, patting my hand with hers. "I'm a huge fan of yours. Something about your artwork speaks to me. I grew up in a small town in the mountains of Montana, surrounded by the kind of scenes you paint. When I read your bio on your website, about how you were the only mixed-race Filipino kid and how people gave you a hard time about it, it hit home."

Her eyes fell to her lap. Even though she didn't say anything, I knew she was thinking back to a time in her past when someone made fun of her for what she looked like—for being different from everyone around her. Just like me.

She cleared her throat, a sad smile playing on her lips. "It's cool to see another half-Filipino kid from the mountains kicking ass. I just want to support that."

Her words immediately eased the wave of nerves hitting my

stomach. Mari Dash may be a celebrity DJ, but she also comes from the same background as me and struggled with the same issues. I was definitely still starstruck by her, but it was easier to see how human and relatable she was.

"Thank you for inviting me," I said. "It means everything. And it means even more to know that you want to support me."

A thunderous beat drop shakes my whole body, pulling me back to the present. I look up and see Mari wink at me as she dances to the frenzied beat of this new song.

"Shay?" A voice calls from behind me.

I spin around and see Colin standing several feet away, eye wide, smiling.

"Holy shit, it *is* you!" He walks over to me and pulls me into a hug.

When we break apart, he shakes his head, still beaming.

"Colin! What are you doing here?"

He glances over at Mari. "I'm a huge fan." His eyes practically dazzle as he stares at her. "My company opened an office in Port-land and we renovated this building before they sold it to the concert venue. They gave us free backstage tickets as a thank you for all the work we did. How did you get back here?"

I explain how Mari bought one of my paintings, Insta-grammed a photo of it, and how that kicked my art business into fifth gear. He offers a heartfelt congratulations.

"Damn, I almost didn't recognize you with your hair short now. Looks nice."

I run a finger along the ends, my face heating when I recall how I decided to chop off most of my hair in a post-breakup stupor.

"I just...needed a change," I say, my eyes falling to the ground. When I look back up at Colin, I notice he's gotten a haircut too. "No more shaggy hair?"

"Gotta look more professional now that I'm taking more client meetings at work. I used to get away with looking as shaggy as Bigfoot. That's what Wes used to say—"

Just the mention of his name sends a lightning bolt to my chest. I try to swallow.

"Shit, I'm sorry, Shay." He squints with embarrassment. "I wasn't even thinking—"

"It's okay. He's your friend. You can talk about him."

Colin shakes his head before tugging on the white button-down he's wearing. "He hasn't been much of one ever since he took off."

I bite my tongue, resisting the urge to ask every question that's been swirling inside of me since the day Wes walked out my door.

Where is he? Does he talk about me? Does he miss me half as much as I miss him? Is he with someone new?

Judging by the pained glance Colin gives me, he can tell exactly what I'm aching to ask.

"I don't know what got into him, Shay. Honestly."

"I don't expect anyone other than him to justify his actions."

He runs a hand through his cropped sandy brown waves. "I just don't know what happened to make him bolt like that."

I contemplate staying silent but talk myself out of it. Colin is Wes's best friend. He deserves to know what happened with him.

I give him a quick summary of how meeting my entire family spooked Wes into a breakup. When I finish, I take a breath, thankful that I didn't get emotional. I haven't spoken about that day in August since sobbing about it to Remy all those months ago.

Colin's response is a wide-eyed stare. "Damn. It all makes sense now."

My chest crushes into itself at what he says. But then he reins in his expression and pats my arm. "Sorry, I didn't mean it like that. It doesn't excuse how he left. You were the best thing that ever happened to him. He told me so."

My heart leaps from my chest to my throat. The need to hear what other lovely things Wes said about me is instinctual. But then I remember where I am.

I'm nearly four months past our breakup. Reminiscing about the good old days won't do me any good. It will just drive the knife in my heart deeper.

I shove aside every urge to ask and shake my head when he tries to speak again.

"None of that matters anymore," I say. "Can you just tell me one thing?"

Colin's face twists in hesitation, but he nods anyway.

"Is he okay? Like, I know he's not my business anymore, but… if you've heard from him, it would just be nice to know that he's, you know…not dead."

I hate how meek and pathetic my shaky voice sounds, but it's the best I can do while battling this wave of nostalgia and emotion.

Colin sighs. "I've spoken to him on the phone. He's doing fine."

Relief courses through me. Wes may have hurt me, but I still care about him as a human being. I still want him to be okay.

"Good." When I say it, I truly mean it. But this one thought, this one mention of Wes is all I'll allow myself. I need to keep focusing on moving forward, on continuing to be the driven, career-focused person I'm working so hard to be.

Colin and I turn back to watch Mari work her magic on her turntable, her hands moving in a graceful symphony.

"Damn, she's something," Colin says. "The way she moves, the kind of music she's making, the way she works a crowd…it's incredible."

I pivot to him, noticing something extra in his gaze. He's not looking at her in awe like the rest of the concert-goers. His stare is of pure admiration. And I recognize it immediately—it's the same way Wes used to look at me.

Colin is more than just a hardcore fanboy of Mari. Something about Mari Dash sets him off in the best way.

An idea pops in my head. "How would you like me to put in a good word for you to Mari?"

Colin's eyes light up as he seems to understand exactly what I'm saying. Pink colors his cheeks, and he shoves his hands in the pockets of his trousers in an adorably bashful move.

"I don't know if I'm her type. She's a celebrity. I'm just a guy who rehabs crumbling buildings."

I smile at him. "She appreciates a down-to-earth mentality more than you'd think. How about I give her your number?"

A wide grin splits his face. "Seriously?"

"I'd be happy to."

CHAPTER TWELVE

I hunch over on my knees on the floor of my apartment, laying out a handful of paintings so they can dry. A loud knock at my door jerks me into a sitting-up position.

"Shay! You in there?" Remy booms.

I stand up and answer the door. He stands, takeout bag in hand. "You didn't answer my text, so surprise lunch delivery it is."

"Sorry, I've been slammed. I haven't had a chance to look at my phone all day."

We side-step around random piles of boxes and paintings until we're at my couch, and plop down.

Remy crinkles his nose. "Have you had a chance to take an honest look at your apartment at all?"

I shove his shoulder, then swipe the food container from his hand. The sweet and savory smell of pad thai hits my nose. My stomach grumbles.

Remy stands up and walks the few feet to the kitchen for two glasses of water. "Damn. I can hear that all the way up here. Have you eaten at all since I saw you last week?"

"Of course I've been eating." I rip open a pair of chopsticks and dig into the noodles. "Just not regularly."

Ever since Mari's concert, I've been busier than before. She took a photo of me signing my artwork in her dressing room, then we took a selfie together after her concert. When she posted those photos on her social media accounts, my orders flew through the roof once more. I spent all of December and January working twelve-hour days to keep up with the orders, only taking Christmas Day and New Year's Eve off to visit my family for a few hours.

"You're looking a bit scrawny these days." Remy settles back next to me and places the glasses on my coffee table.

I roll my eyes while chewing.

"I'm serious," Remy says, digging into his own noodles. "Look, there's no one who's more excited than me about your business taking off. But you can't neglect yourself. Remember what happened last time?"

I direct my dagger-stare from Remy to my pad thai. "I don't know what you're talking about."

"Come on. You and I both know that post-breakup Shay is not the Shay we want."

Dropping my container on the coffee table, I reach for a glass and down some water, hoping my silence conveys that I don't want to talk about my sorry post-breakup state, especially when I feel so good about where I'm at now.

Remy leans over, taking a whiff of my hair. "You smell like coconut and verbena, not BO, so at least you're bathing regularly again."

I elbow his arm, but all he does is chuckle.

"How are things at Dandy Lime?" I ask.

He takes my cue to move on. "Busy. We miss you working there, but seeing you live out your dreams makes me all sorts of happy."

The knot inside of me eases at Remy's kind words. "I'm sorry I haven't worked a shift lately, but I had to devote all my time to this."

Remy nods and we finish our last few bites. He collects our empty containers and tosses them in the trash, then stands in front of me, hands on his hips.

I frown up at him. "What?"

"We both know what day is coming up."

I say nothing, choosing to ignore that in a few days it will be Valentine's Day—the day that I met Wes almost a year ago.

Remy sighs, his expression turning tender. "I just wanted to make sure you weren't getting down about it."

"I'm not. I'm fine."

It's a half-lie. When I'm distracted with work, I *do* feel fine. But when I think about how happy I was a year ago—and how it all came crashing down—I can't help but feel sad.

"I get what you're doing," Remy says. "You're distracting yourself with work. But you have to be more than just a workaholic, Shay. Work-life balance is important. You'll drive yourself into the ground if you're not careful."

I open my mouth to object, but I come up with nothing. He's right.

"You should go out more, run errands, have a drink at your handsome cousin's bar, flirt—"

"Really, Remy? Flirt?"

A soft smile tugs at Remy's lips and he pats my leg. "Yes, even flirting."

I bite back a groan, but the annoyed sound still seeps out. "If I promise to get out of the apartment, will you stop giving me unsolicited life advice?"

"I make no guarantees, but I'll do my best."

I laugh. "Fine."

When I pop into the bookstore down the street from Remy's bar, I'm greeted with an instrumental rendition of an old Michael

Bolton hit. I chuckle as I slowly trot through the stacks, stopping whenever I see a book that catches my eye.

It's strange being out in the middle of the day like this when I've got a mountain of projects to finish, but I promised Remy I'd get out for a least a little while today.

I swipe a romance novel from the top shelf, tapping my toe along to the beat of the power ballad.

"You're a Michael Bolton fan I take it?"

I twist my head to the voice and am greeted with a pleasant visual. Tall, broad, blond, late-twenties, with a killer pair of blue eyes and an equally lethal smile.

Heat makes its way up my cheeks and I smile to myself as my gaze falls to the floor. I turn back to him. "You busted me."

"I confess that I sing along to his songs while driving in the car." He swipes a thriller from a nearby shelf. "Windows always up though, obviously."

"Obviously."

We share a laugh. He gestures to the book in my hand, which displays a particularly delicious and well-oiled six-pack. "So, Michael Bolton and romance novels are your guilty pleasures then?"

"There is absolutely no reason to feel guilty about reading a romance novel."

He holds his hand up in playful defense. "Message received." His hands fall back to his side, his gaze lingering on me an extra second longer. "I was only kidding, by the way. My mom and sister love romance. And I think people should read whatever makes them happy."

"I agree." I pause, letting my gaze linger on his bright blue eyes. This friendly chit-chat feels dangerously close to flirting. Remy would be proud.

I take a step toward him. "So what's your favorite romance novel?"

"I have to confess, I haven't read any." He leans forward.

"You should. They're a lot of fun."

I bump the book in his hand with my book. He bites his lip while chuckling. Crossing the touch barrier breaks the last bit of self-consciousness holding me back. He's full-on smiling now.

"We could start a book club," he says. "You introduce me to your favorite romances and I'll show you my favorite thrillers?"

I stare up at him and shrug. "Maybe."

Still smiling, he raises an eyebrow at me. "How about a drink first?"

"I'll need your name before I agree to that."

He sticks out his hand, that killer smile still on display. "I'm Garret."

I clasp his hand in mind. Inside I'm buzzing at the soft warmth of skin-on-skin. It's been forever.

"Shay. It's nice to meet you. Now about that drink. How about tomorrow? It's Valentine's Day after all."

Just the mention of the day has me hesitant because of all those memories of Wes—both good and awful. But then I blink, determined not to let him taint this day for me forever.

I force a smile at Garret. "Tomorrow sounds perfect."

CHAPTER THIRTEEN

Three days after Wes came back into my life and screwed everything up

I'm on the floor of my apartment on my hands and knees, finishing my latest work. It's not a cityscape or a landscape watercolor or a sketch. It's just splotches of whatever paint I have on hand. I glance around the room and check the other dozen splotchy works I have drying on the floor.

Locking myself in my apartment to paint nonstop for days probably isn't the healthiest way to cope after Wes popped back into my life out of the blue, but it's better than falling apart. Better than sobbing while lying on the floor, something I refuse to do. I spent months working my way back to my strong, resilient self—the person I was before my breakup with Wes. I know that I'm her again because instead of crying, I'm painting. I've wasted enough tears on Wes Paulsen. There will be no more. I'll make sure of it.

Pounding on my door yanks me out of my paint-filled stupor. "Shay, it's Remy. Let me in."

I huff a sigh, stand up, and open the door.

"What is going on?" Remy frowns down at me. "Why did you go off the grid again?" He scans the floor. "What the..." He turns to face me, then grabs me by the shoulders, forcing me to look at him. "What the hell happened to make you go into Jackson Pollock hermit mode?"

"I'm not Jackson Pollock, and I'm not a hermit." I shrug out of his hold. "I'm doing just fine."

He raises an eyebrow at me. "Seriously?"

I shake my head and plop onto the couch. The moment my body hits the plush cushioning, my muscles relax. Remy's soft footsteps follow behind me.

I rest my hands on my knees. "Look. I'm going to tell you something, but you can't freak out."

Remy's brow wrinkles. "Okay..."

"Wes is back. I saw him. At Dandy Lime the other night."

Remy's jaw falls opens so fast, I wince at the popping sound the sudden movement makes.

"No freaking way." He rubs my arm. "Crap, cuz. I'm sorry, I—"

I shake my head. "Don't be sorry. I'm fine."

Again, he raises an eyebrow at me. "You're fine?"

I nod. Remy gestures to the mess of paintings on my floor.

"I refuse to cry over him anymore. I'm working instead."

Remy scoots next to me. "Shay, it's okay to be sad."

"I'm not sad." My voice reaches that hard tone that always hits when I'm annoyed.

"No, I mean...okay, don't get me wrong. I'm so happy that you're not crying over him anymore. But try not to shove your feelings aside."

"I'm not." My tone comes off harder than I mean it to.

"All I'm saying is that sometimes you can think you're okay, but then something happens to set you off. It's happened to me before."

I quietly soak in his words.

"Wes was a big part of your life, Shay. And he hurt you. It's awesome to see you strong like always, but a random wave of sadness or frustration can hit. It'll be easier to weather if you acknowledge it instead of just trying to suppress everything."

My gaze falls to my lap. Everything Remy says is true.

"That's good advice, Remy. Thank you."

He slips his arm around me, cuddling me into his chest. I melt into his hold, thankful that despite all my proclamations of strength, my cousin knows I could use a hug right now.

"What, no lecturing me about faking it till I make it?" I say.

"You're doing just fine. If one of my exes had left me the way Wes left you, then showed back up unannounced a year to the day we met—on Valentine's Day of all days—I would have spent a week on the floor curled up in the fetal position."

I laugh and lean against Remy's shoulder, closing my eyes. Against the darkness, I see Wes in a crystal-clear flashback from days ago. His tousled hair, his close-cropped beard, those rich brown eyes riddled with sorrow. No matter how strong I try to be, I can't deny how I'm still physically attracted to Wes.

"He looked good, Remy," I groan. "So damn good."

"Bastard."

I open my eyes and grab my phone from the coffee table. I sort through the missed calls and messages from Remy, then focus on what's left.

One missed call, one voicemail, and one text message.

"I bet I know who those are from," Remy says.

I stare at the screen until it fades to black. "Part of me wants to delete these without even looking at them."

"I can do that for you, you know," Remy says. "I'll delete all of them so you don't have to deal with them."

I hold my breath. "No. I can do this on my own."

I type in my passcode, then listen to the voicemail first.

"Shay."

Just the sound of Wes's low tone and gravelly register makes my insides implode. He sighs deeply. When I blink, I can picture the wrinkle of his brow, how he's clenching his jaw when he pauses.

"I know I have no right to come back into your life like this, but…"

Another long exhale. My entire body hums and it feels like betrayal. It's practically a reflex how every part of me begs to be close to him at just the sound of his voice. I force myself to focus back on the moment.

"…I just want to talk, that's all. Just give me a chance to explain myself, to let me say sorry in person. Please, babe?"

I punch the phone into the couch cushion next to me. Remy jerks back.

I roll my eyes. "Oh please, I know you could hear it. Don't even try to pretend otherwise."

"True, and that's exactly why I'm confused. What about his message made you so angry?"

Something hot settles under my skin. I can feel the heat all the way from my feet to my cheeks. "He has no right to call me babe. Not after how he left me."

I swallow back the fire burning in my chest, the flames licking at the base of my throat.

"That's fair," Remy says. "Do you want to read his text?"

I shake my head, then hand my phone to him. "No. Delete it for me. Please."

"You sure?"

"Erase it. Now."

Remy offers a solemn nod. I take a sip of water, looking up at him. He stares down at the screen, carries out my order, and sets my phone back on the coffee table. "It's done."

"Thank you," I say quietly.

He grabs my hand. "Come bartend for me."

"Remy, we've been over this. I'm too busy with work, I don't have time."

"You had time to go off the grid and shellac a dozen blank canvases with every kind of paint."

I cross my arms, scowling at them. "I was working."

"It would be good for you to spend a few hours every night away from your apartment."

I start to object, but he cuts me off.

"You can make time to sling a few drinks. Don't even try to tell me it's not possible."

Instead of arguing I say nothing, refusing to admit he's right. Bartending for a couple of hours a few times a week would be easy to work in.

But that would open myself up to the risk of seeing Wes in person. He's already tried to catch me there once. I have no doubt he'll try again.

I bite back the groan of disappointment I'm aching to let loose. "What if he comes into the bar?"

"Then I'll throw him out."

"That simple, huh?"

"I'll make it that simple. I promise."

I inhale. "Okay. I'll do it."

CHAPTER FOURTEEN

a week of bartending in the evenings and Wes is a no-show. I'd be lying if I said I wasn't surprised. I half-expected him to crawl through the entrance of Dandy Lime on his hands and knees, begging for my forgiveness. But he apparently has better things to do.

Remy slides up next to me, wiping down the counter with a towel. "How are you holding up?"

"Fine."

It's only half-true. Part of me is fine that Wes hasn't shown his face here. But the other part of me is wondering when exactly I'll see him again. I can't live in this holding pattern forever.

Remy frowns. I know he doesn't believe a word I've said. But he's gracious and doesn't call me on it. He leaves me with a pat on the shoulder before turning to the next customer at the bar and taking their order.

I check the clock. Five minutes to last call. I do a run-through of the tables, swiping up any empty glasses, then shout the warning for last call.

I'm restacking napkins when out of the corner of my eye someone walks over.

"What can I get you?" I ask, still fixated on the dispenser.

"Tequila, please."

My hands freeze when the rough, low voice hits my ears. I don't have to look up. I know it's Wes.

Instead of serving him, I stay standing in place.

Seconds pass. Wes clears his throat. "Could we maybe..."

"No."

It bursts from my mouth like a soft-spoken bullet. Every muscle in my body tenses. The last time I let Wes in, it broke me. Never, ever again.

"I just want to talk," Wes says.

When I finally look up at him, he's just as sad as he sounds. His brow is furrowed, his shoulders are slumped, and his rich brown eyes are a new shade of sorrowful. Still so damn handsome, though. There's a squeeze at the center of my chest where my heart used to be, where it used to beat just for him.

I swallow the pain back. "You wanna talk over tequila? Are you serious right now?"

Our conversation nabs the attention of a handful of nearby patrons. Heavy footsteps echo behind me.

"I think you should leave," Remy says from behind me.

Wes's pained stare darts to right above my head. He opens his mouth to speak, but Remy cuts him off. "Leave now or I'll make you leave."

Wes sighs, the hesitation evident in the way his eyes dart around, then back at me. "I'm really not trying to cause a scene. All I want is to talk."

"She already told you she's not interested," Remy says.

Another loaded silence. The background noise of chatter and laughing has died out. Instead, there are hushed whispers. Heat crawls up my chest, my neck, my cheeks. Everyone is watching our charged exchange.

Wes tries again, but Remy shuts him down. I wonder just how long this will play out. Will Wes leave me alone for a stretch of days, then show up at the bar, pleading for a chance to talk? At that rate, I'll never, ever get over him. Maybe a final talk is what I need to close this chapter of our past for good, and then I can move on. We both can.

I place a hand on Remy's arm. "It's fine."

He backs away a few steps and clears the empties from the bar top.

I pivot back to Wes. "We close in twenty minutes. Come back then and we'll talk."

The tiniest glimmer hits Wes's eyes. A second later he blinks, and his face is serious again. "I'll be here."

∾

"You sure you don't need me to stay with you?" Remy asks while cashing out the register.

"I appreciate the offer, but I'll be fine. I promise." I prop the last chair on top of the last table. "You can wait in the office."

"Fine." He practically growls it.

There's a soft whoosh sound when the door opens. I look up. Wes again. For a few seconds, all we do is stand and stare at each other, as if we didn't just see and talk to each other twenty minutes ago.

I swallow and gesture for him to take a seat at the bar.

Remy shoots me one last look, but I shake my head. He stomps to his office in the back, shutting the door behind him.

I walk over to the bar and stand across from Wes. "Tequila, right?"

"Yes, please."

"What kind?"

"Whatever kind you want to give me."

His tone is so soft, so pleading, I nearly break. But I keep my focus on the task. I contemplate serving him the lowest quality swill we have, but that bottle is practically empty and I don't want to open a new one just for him. Yes, it's petty, but I can't help it. Six months ago this man left me a sobbing heap on the floor of my apartment. Downing that nail polish remover masquerading as tequila would be a lenient punishment.

I sigh, opting for a bottle of Jose Cuervo, pour it in the glass, then slide it to him.

"What do you have to say, Wes?" There's no need for pleasantries, not with a history like ours.

"Your hair. It's short now. It looks really pretty."

"Save it." I bite my tongue to keep from yelling. Compliments are not allowed between us right now...or ever again.

"I'm so, so sorry." Everything in his tone, in his face, reads sorrow. It's not enough, though.

"For what?" I want to bark the question, but I strain to keep my voice at a respectable tone.

He clears his throat, glancing down at his drink for a second before answering me. "For everything."

"Try again."

He clears his throat. "I'm sorry for how I hurt you, for the things I said, for the way I left. I wish I could take it all back."

I swallow back another quip, letting the silence dance between us.

"I'm sorry I didn't try to contact you when I left. I just didn't know how to make things right." He takes a sip and pauses to breathe. "But I'm back now. For good."

He waits like he's expecting me to say something. I say nothing.

His face falls. "I'm...you'll never know just how sorry I am, Shay."

Pursing my lips is the only way I can get the lump in my throat to keep from growing into a full-fledged sob. Remy was right; emotions can hit when you least expect—at the exact moment you don't want them to. I may not have cried over Wes these past couple of weeks, but I suspect I'm about to make up for it now. All that anger, sadness, and frustration from before comes tumbling back like an invisible tsunami leveling my insides. My eyes water, but thankfully no tears fall—yet. I spin around and pretend to dry a glass while I silently deep-breathe, hoping I can keep from crying in Wes's presence.

"Shay," he practically whispers. "Talk to me. Please."

I close my eyes. I can barely handle how sincere he sounds. Still, I stand, my back to him, still saying nothing.

"How...how were things with you?" he asks.

"How do you think they were?"

"Shay, I said I was sorry."

Fire bursts through me. I spin around, glaring at him. "Are you fucking kidding me right now? You think you can just come back, toss a few apologies in my face, and that makes it all better?"

His frown takes on a confused shine. "What? No. That's not—"

"How the hell did you think I felt after I told you I loved you and you walked out on me?"

My voice booms against the exposed brick.

The office door squeaks open just enough for Remy to peek his head out. "Everything okay?"

"It's fine!" I yell.

Crossing my arms, I aim my death glare back at Wes. He stares, eyes wide.

"I loved you so much, Wes. And you just left, like I never meant anything to you."

I speak through sobs. His hand slides across the bar, but I step out of his reach.

"You think coming back with a half-assed apology makes it all good?"

His mouth falls open, but no words come out.

I wipe my face on my sleeves and scoff. "Seriously, Wes. Screw you."

When I glimpse his face, it's red. With anger, with hurt, with frustration, I don't really know and I don't really care. All I know is that agreeing to meet with him was a mistake. Yes, he said sorry. But that's just a word, a drop in the bottomless bucket of tears I cried for him when he left.

I spin around, swipe my coat from behind the counter, and dart out the door.

"Shay, wait!" he calls from behind.

I stomp down the sidewalk, ignoring the sleet pelleting my face. Why the hell didn't I bring my hat? I squeeze my hands into fists, realizing then that I don't have my mittens either. It's the end of February for god's sake.

"Cuz! Where are you going?"

Shoving my hands in my pockets, I ignore Remy's calls and walk straight ahead in the exact opposite direction of my apartment, with no particular destination in mind.

"Shay!" Wes booms from behind.

Fresh tears freeze the second they touch my cheeks thanks to the biting arctic wind. I try to pick up my pace, but the sleet has turned the concrete below into an ice rink. I wobble for a second, then steady myself, stepping forward with renewed caution. Just then I feel a firm hand on my arm, turning me around.

"Would you just stop for one second and listen to me?"

Wes's pained eyes stare back at me. His dark brown hair glistens as the icy rain falls on his uncovered head.

"I'm done listening to you." I jerk out of his grip.

He shakes his head. "You think I wasn't heartbroken too when I left? I was a mess. I could see that I hurt you and that killed me. I didn't call or text because I didn't know what to say."

His eyes glimmer. My throat squeezes. He's trying not to cry. But one thing sticks out, one word is missing in all that he says: love. And that's the problem.

Wes may have been heartbroken too, but that doesn't take away the one key difference between us: I loved him—I still love him. But he never loved me.

My breath catches when I try to keep a sob from ripping free.

"Reeling from a breakup is awful. But do you know what's worse? Telling someone you love them and watching them walk out on you."

Frozen raindrops hit my skin like needles as I wait for him to respond. But there's nothing. Just his silence and his presence, both reminders of what I wanted most in the world but couldn't have. Because he didn't want it.

"Shay, I—"

"Stop," I bark. "I don't know why you even came back."

I spin around and jog ahead, hoping the slickness of the sidewalks discourages him from following. I pick up speed, ignoring the burn in my legs, ignoring the rational part of my brain that's telling me to slow down, that it's too damn icy for me to be running in my knock-off Ugg boots.

But I shove aside that voice, letting my legs lead the way. Wes didn't come back to make things right with me. He came back to clear his conscience.

I run and run and run until my lungs are on fire, my hair and face dripping with icy rain. And then I lose my footing on a slick spot. My feet fly out from under me the second I lose my balance. I hit the pavement back-first. All I see are stars.

CHAPTER FIFTEEN

*T*wo sets of hands gently grip both of my arms, hauling me up to my feet. I blink until the stars turn to actual images. Remy stands to my right and Wes stands to my left. They steady me, then hit me with dual concerned stares.

"I told you to stop," Wes says once I'm back on my feet.

"And I told you to go away," I snap.

Remy shushes us both. "Can you two save your lovers' quarrel until we can figure out if Shay is okay?"

"I'm fine," I bark.

But just as I speak the words, pain shoots through my left ankle and my left wrist. When I try to put my weight on my left leg, I nearly fall, but Remy and Wes hold me in place. I grip Wes's coat sleeve with my left hand, wincing at the pressure in my wrist.

"Easy," Wes says.

I wince through gritted teeth. "I think it's my ankle. And wrist."

He and Remy exchange concerned frowns, then Remy pulls up the rideshare app on his phone.

"What are you doing?" I ask.

"Getting you home."

"Remy, I live a mile in the other direction. I don't need a car to take me."

"You can barely walk, Shay. No way you're walking a mile in your state."

"I can carry her."

Remy and I both whip our heads to Wes. "What?" we say in unison.

"I'll carry her to her apartment," Wes repeats.

"No way," I say.

Remy shakes his head. "Do you see how slick the concrete is? That's just what we need, you slipping on ice so you fall down and injure yourself and Shay."

Wes mutters something, but it's so low in volume I can't understand it. Soon, a car pulls up and the three of us get in. We share a silent two-minute ride together until we halt at the front of my building.

Remy leads me to the front door but Wes stops him. "I can make sure she gets up there okay. You still need to lock up the bar, don't you?"

The conflict plays out on Remy's face, clear enough for me and Wes to see. Stay here and be the honorable cousin taking care of me but risk getting his unlocked bar robbed.

I huff out a frustrated breath at the thought of Wes setting foot in my apartment. The last time he was there marked the end for us.

But he's right. I'm going to need help making it up the stairs.

"It's okay, Remy," I say.

Remy shoots wide eyes at me, but I pat his shoulder. "I promise, I'm good. Wes is right, you need to get back to the bar and lock up." I tug on the hem of my coat, aware that I'm the cause of tonight's chaos. "It's my fault. If I hadn't—"

Wes shakes his head. "If it's anyone's fault, it's mine. I upset you, and that's why you ran off."

Remy slow-blinks, zipping his coat all the way up to his chin.

"Well, now that we've played the blame game, I'm off." He turns to me. "Text me when you're settled in your apartment okay? And let me know if you need anything. I can come right over when I'm done."

I clear my throat. "I'll pay you back for the ride later, okay."

"Don't even worry about it." Remy turns his darkened stare to Wes. "Take care of her."

He crosses the street just as Wes bends down to scoop me up.

"What the hell are you doing?" I try to wiggle out of his hold, but he has me firmly against him.

He kicks the entrance door open, then starts the three-story trudge to my door. "Carrying you." He says it without a single labored breath.

"Why?"

"Because you're hurt and it's my fault."

I have nothing to say to that. Instead, I focus on the feel of his hot breath hitting a sliver of exposed skin on my chest, right above where my zipper came undone when I slipped on the ice. That tiny hint of contact awakens my senses. I soak in the heat of each exhale as it hits my skin, the way his hard body feels pressed against mine.

We make it to my door and he's barely broken a sweat. He sets me down, I unlock the door, and take a step inside. And then he scoops me back up and heads for the couch.

"Watch out for—"

"The dip in the floor," he says, cutting me off. "I remember."

I swallow hard as he sets me on the couch. The fact that he remembers makes me feel like I mean something, like I still matter to him—even though I know I don't.

I focus instead on shoving off my coat.

"Let me." He kneels next to me and my entire body flushes. It's as if I didn't just stand outside for ten solid minutes in the freezing rain. I feel so hot at his presence, at the prospect of his touch.

113

With gentle hands, he pulls off my coat, then my shoes.

His dark eyes connect with mine. "Your clothes are soaking wet."

"You're not going to change me."

He turns away just as I catch the beginnings of an eye roll. He pads to my dresser on the other side of my apartment, returning with some yoga pants, a hoodie, and wool socks.

Before I can demand that he turn around, he heads straight for the bathroom and shuts the door. I do the quickest change I can manage with a throbbing wrist and ankle.

"Decent!" I call out to him.

He emerges with an ace bandage in hand and sits on the coffee table. "What hurts more, your ankle or your wrist?"

"What are you doing?"

"Helping you." His brow furrows, clearly put off by my question.

"Did it occur to you to ask if I want your help in the first place?"

My phone buzzes, interrupting our frown-off. A text from Remy.

Remy: *You make it inside okay?*

Me: *Yes. Wes is helping me get settled.*

Remy: *Want me to stop by?*

"Shay."

I glance up at Wes, his frown now softer.

"I'm the reason you got hurt. Please let me take care of you. It's the least I can do."

I swallow. "What exactly will that entail?"

Twenty minutes ago I was raging at Wes, but I'm not exactly in a position to turn him down now. And I've inconvenienced Remy enough for one night. I don't want him to spend his evening checking up on me when he should be sleeping.

Wes rubs his jaw. "It would entail me wrapping your ankle or your wrist—whichever hurts worse because I can only find one ace bandage in your bathroom. Then I'll carry you to your bed so you can sleep. I'll take the couch."

I start to object, but he shakes his head.

"You might have hit your head when you fell. Do you remember if you did or not?"

I shake my head no.

"And I'm guessing you'd shoot down my suggestion to take you to the hospital to get checked out."

"Yup," I answer, the faintest hint of bitterness in my tone.

"Then you need someone here to keep an eye on you to make you sure you don't have a head injury or something serious. Just for tonight."

When I don't say anything in response, he sighs. "I just want to make sure you're okay."

One night. One night of my ex sleeping on my couch, four feet away from me, after his request for a chat turned into a horrible argument.

I let out a soft exhale. "The pain in my wrist is starting to ease up, but my ankle's still throbbing. Can you please wrap it?"

He nods, then kneels in front of me. He slides my sock off, then softly rests his hands on my bare ankle. I swallow, ordering my senses to keep it together. There's nothing personal about this touch. It's all business.

And it's happening because he hurt me—because he thinks he owes me.

I text Remy that I'll be fine without him. He texts that he'll check on me in the morning.

Wes wraps the bandage tightly around my ankle, then slips the sock back on. "Ready for bed?"

"I need to brush my teeth first."

He scoops me up and carries me to the bathroom before I can utter a word of protest. When I'm finished, he carries me to the bed, then props a pillow under my ankle. Then he fetches me an aspirin and a glass of water. I mutter a thank you.

"Just yell if you need anything," he says. The way he stares down at me tests my renewed resolve. His gaze is watchful, tender, and almost too much.

I fixate on my ankle to distract myself. "Okay."

He turns out the lights, then settles on the couch. The rustling of fabric fills the silent space. I close my eyes, imagining him taking his clothes off in the darkness.

My throat aches with the knowledge at how none of this means anything to him...and how it means everything to me.

Minutes pass. I know I should be trying to sleep, but I speak up anyway.

"Wes?" My voice is a sharp whisper.

"Yeah?"

He sounds alert when he speaks. I exhale, relieved that I didn't wake him. "Thank you."

"No. Thank you, Shay."

With those final words, I fall asleep.

THE SOFT SOUNDS of metal hitting ceramic wake me. I open my eyes and peek up at Wes standing in my tiny kitchen, stirring a cup of coffee.

For a split second his brow jumps to his hairline, but then it eases back to its rightful place. My chest squeezes at the sight of him in my apartment...that used to be *our* apartment.

"Sorry, did I wake you?" he asks.

"It's fine. You made coffee and that's exactly what I need right now." I push myself up to a sitting position and feel the tell-tale pressure of my bladder. I clear my throat. "After I, um..."

I look at the bathroom. Wes drops the spoon on the counter and jogs over to me.

"Right, you're probably dying to pee. Sorry."

Like some sort of firefighter on a romance novel cover, he

hauls me up with zero effort like last night and walks me to the bathroom. When I'm finished, I hobble the three feet to the kitchen counter just as he tries to reach for me.

"I've got it, Wes."

"You really shouldn't stress your ankle." He stares at my ankle while he speaks.

Leaning against the counter, I blow on my mug of coffee, then take a careful sip. "I'll survive, I'm sure."

He crosses his arms, leaning on the wall across from me. It's a strangely foreign stance we take in this space where a handful of months ago we couldn't keep our hands off each other.

He turns his head to glance at the far end of the counter. I stare too, and then immediately dart my eyes away, remembering we had stand-up sex at that exact spot a month before he left me.

Wes clears his throat. From behind my mug, I peek up at him. His eyes are shy and his cheeks are crimson. Looks like that memory hit him, too.

"So," he says after another handful of awkward silent seconds. "How long until you think you'll be ready?"

"Ready for what?"

"For me to take you to the hospital to get your wrist and your ankle checked out?"

I shake my head. "I'm not doing that."

Just then my phone, which is still on my nightstand, rings. I turn and start to walk toward it, but Wes tells me to rest and finish my coffee while he gets it.

"It's your mom," he says, sliding his finger across the screen to answer it before I can even tell him to ignore it.

"Hi, Mom."

"Anak! Remy said you fell and hurt yourself last night. Are you okay?"

I grit my teeth, annoyed. Hopefully, Remy left out the part that Wes was involved at all. If she finds out he's here, she'll drive all the way from Redmond to lay into him for breaking my heart, and that's the last thing I need to deal with.

"I'm fine, Mom."

"Nonsense."

Car keys jingle in the background.

"I'll take you to the doctor and then when we get home I'll cook you some *biko*. That was your favorite dessert when you were little, remember? Always made you feel better, no matter how upset you were about anything."

Despite my mom's overbearing response, my mouth waters at just the mention of that sticky rice cake, the perfect combination of coconut milk, glutinous rice, and brown sugar. I can't have her babying me though. If I don't stop her, she'll fuss over me for weeks.

"Mom, I don't need you to come here."

"You need to go to the hospital," she says with absolute certainty, as if she hasn't heard me at all.

There's no use in arguing, so instead I opt for a little white lie. "I'm already going, you don't need to come. The doctor will examine me and send me home to rest. I promise I'll let you know if I need anything."

"Who's taking you?"

"A friend."

The hard clank of her car keys hitting the side table near the entryway of her front door signals that I've stopped her. Thankfully.

"Okay. That sounds fine then."

I thank her, and she tells me she whip up some *biko* for me and drop it off tomorrow. When I hand up, Wes points his frown at me. "Now are you ready to go?"

"I'm not going, Wes. I just said that to keep my mom from freaking out."

"Shay, don't be stubborn."

"Then don't be ridiculous, Wes."

My voice is harsher than I mean for it to be. But it's barely eight a.m., my ankle and wrist are throbbing, and I'm staving off my worried mom all the while standing across from my ex-boyfriend when all I want is to be alone. I've got almost no patience for this.

"I'll be fine. I just need to rest." I take a long breath. It barely soothes me.

He raises a judgmental eyebrow at me. "That's not going to fly with me. Or your mom."

"Fortunately, neither one of you is in charge of me, so you don't have to worry about that."

I take a final gulp of coffee, set the empty mug on the counter, and twist myself around to walk into the living room, but Wes's gentle hand on my arm stops me. "Just listen to me for a sec, okay?"

I shrug out of his grip, but stay in place. His chest heaves with the slow breath he takes, like he's just now remembering that I get notoriously impatient when I'm fussed over.

"I understand that you don't want to be around me. But you're hurt, Shay. You'll be a million times worse off if you ignore your injury and try to power through it. Think about how that will slow you down with your workload."

I squint at him. "How do you know about my workload?"

His expression softens. "I um, I heard about how your business blew up while I was away. I saw Mari Dash's Instagram post about you."

I purse my lips to keep my jaw from dropping to the ground. How in the world would he know about that? He's been off-the-grid hiking for six months. Instagram, social media, all that should have been the furthest thing from his mind.

"How? Weren't you in the mountains with no cell service this whole time?"

He opens his mouth, then clamps it shut. "I was, but..." he

shakes his head. "I'd got into town sometimes. I looked you up a couple times."

Warmth hits my chest as he speaks the words. I must have been on his mind a tiny bit if he knows about my business blowing up. But another thought sinks in. He put in the effort to check up on me online, but never called or texted me.

I shake my head, swallowing back the quip I ache to unleash on him. The last thing I need is another blow-out in my apartment.

"I managed just fine without you for the past six months," I mutter, eyes on the ground. "I'm sure I can do it again."

All that follows is a sharp intake of breath. "Shay."

The softness in his tone compels me to look up at him. "I know you hate me right now. You have every right to. But don't make your work suffer because of me." He clears his throat. "You've been commissioned for a bunch of projects, right? Which means you have loads of packages to mail every week, emails to keep up with, orders to take, and keeping your home studio organized, right?"

I nod.

"You can't do all that work with an injury, especially if you refuse to treat it. The sooner you get checked out, the sooner you can dive back into work. Tell me that's not what you want."

I nod because he's right. Diving back into work, distracting myself from this mess we've currently found ourselves in is exactly what I want. And to do that, I need to be well.

"Okay," I say, my voice rough in sound but soft in volume. "You can help me."

"Let me take you to get checked out then."

I catch myself before I nod my agreement. I deserve some answers first. "Wait."

"What is it?" he asks, frowning.

"Why are you so hell-bent on helping me?"

"I upset you last night with my sorry-ass excuse for an apology. It's what caused you to run off and get hurt. I owe it to you."

"It's more than that. I can tell."

He rubs his hands over his jaw. I let my gaze linger over the beautiful angles and hard edges that make up his face, that deliciously well-groomed beard. I'm silently, shamefully admiring how ruggedly handsome it makes him.

"Honestly?" he asks.

"Honestly."

This time when he looks at me, his gaze is piercing, like he can see right through me to my insides, to all the feelings and emotions swirling inside of me.

"Because I spent months missing you so hard, I ached from the inside out. I'll take any excuse to see you, even though I don't deserve it. Even though I know you hate me."

I respond with silence, my head spinning. Not once does his stare leave mine during the few quiet seconds we share.

"And honestly Shay, I have the tiniest suspicion that despite everything you say, despite how you feel about me right now, you want me here, too."

He moves past me to my dresser, leaving me speechless.

CHAPTER SIXTEEN

"It looks like you've got pretty severe sprains in your left wrist and left ankle," the doctor at the urgent care says.

He studies the x-rays of my wrist. A second later he switches it out to the x-ray of my ankle, resuming his serious face.

"But they're not broken, right?" I ask.

"That's correct."

Wes clears his throat. This whole time he's been by my side as I navigated the waiting room, the paperwork, the two-hour-long process of taking x-rays, and waiting for the doctor. He's dialed back his instinct to pick me up and carry me everywhere, thankfully. Instead, he's just hovering close by.

Half of me is annoyed. We're not together and he's acting like a protective bodyguard—like a boyfriend.

But half of me appreciates the thought. Because what he said earlier was true. As much as the other half of me still resents him for how he left all those months ago, my other half—the half that instinctively relaxes at his touch, his voice, his presence—is happy he's here.

"But she's okay?" Wes asks.

The doctor nods. "Other than a few weeks of taking it easy while recovering, Shay will be just fine."

My ears perk up at the mention of "a few weeks." I squirm while sitting in the exam room bed, my movement causing the paper lining underneath me to crinkle so loudly, it echoes in the tiny exam room.

"What exactly does 'taking it easy' entail?" I ask.

The doctor pulls a couple of ace bandages from a nearby drawer and hands them to me. "For starters, keeping your wrist and your ankle wrapped. And keep them elevated as much as you can. It also looks like you have a slight avulsion in your wrist."

"Avulsion?" Wes and I say in unison.

The doctor nods, consulting my chart. "That just means a bit of bone has been pulled from your wrist when you sprained it. It should heal on its own, but you shouldn't stress it. That means no typing, no repetitive movements, no writing, playing racquet sports, no lifting, anything like that."

My head spins as he lists off more activities I can't do.

"For your ankle, that means no exercise for the next few weeks. And when you walk, use a crutch with your good arm to keep the stress off the injury."

I can't speak. Wes seems to read my silence for the panicked gesture that it truly is.

"She's an artist," he says. "She stands sometimes when she paints and sketches."

The doctor shrugs, clearly unmoved by Wes's explanation. He turns to me. "Sorry, but those are your instructions for recovery. If you want to avoid permanently injuring yourself, you need to take it seriously. You should be fine to ease back into minor activities in three or four weeks."

He leaves the room while we wait for a nurse to come back with my paperwork. My head spins.

"But...I have so much work to do."

"I know," Wes says.

"I was commissioned to do this multi-panel canvas work. I have revisions for a children's book I'm illustrating. I...I have sketches that need polishing and digital projects that I haven't even started yet. I'm on deadline."

When my voice starts to shake, Wes grips me by the shoulders. "Shay."

I fix my stare on him. Suddenly everything is steady.

"It'll be okay. You can contact your clients and explain that you've had a health emergency and will have to deliver their projects a few weeks late. They'll understand."

"Will they?" I practically scoff my response. "I worked so hard for so long trying to get myself to this point—where I'm supporting myself with my art. And now that I've just barely made it, I'm about to lose it all."

If I blow this opportunity, it's back to soul-sucking office jobs and staying up till the wee hours of the morning completing art projects. No way do I want that again.

"You won't lose it all. Don't even think that." Wes speaks with such authority, I almost believe him. "Your clients want your work. You're a sought-after artist now, remember? Waiting a few extra weeks won't make a bit of difference to them, I promise."

"How can you promise something like that?"

I bite my tongue at my bitter tone. I still can't stand that he followed me online after he left. It's such a sneaky thing to do. He could have just called. He could have just texted. He could have just—

My cheeks heat. But he didn't. And I need to remember that every time my brain goes crazy with all the things I wish Wes could have done.

I swallow, willing the hurt and frustration to stay below the surface where it belongs.

Releasing me, he takes a seat in the stool across from the exam table. A vein I never noticed before bulges in his neck.

"Disobeying doctor's orders and permanently screwing up

your wrist and ankle just because you're obnoxiously stubborn doesn't seem like the smartest thing to do, does it?"

Tension flashes between us like a bolt of lightning.

"Wes, I just got career-altering news. Can you just let me have a minute to process it all?"

He runs a hand through his hair. "You won't be doing this alone," he says. "I'll be there to help you."

"How, exactly?"

The huff of breath he lets out is riddled with frustration. I can tell by his frown, by the clench of his jaw, how his hands fall to rest at his waist. I hardly ever saw it when we were together. But now that we're exes thrust together by a weird set of circumstances, frustration seems to be his default. My stomach churns at the thought that I'm the cause.

I used to make him so happy.

I wipe the thought away, focusing instead on his expression.

"I'm suggesting that I help you in your daily tasks," he says.

"What are you going to do, paint for me?"

He rolls his eyes. "Do you have to take that tone?"

"How am I supposed to sound? I just got the news that for the next three weeks I can't use my leg or my arm."

Wes glances down, then back at me. This time the frustration is dialed back. A sliver of tenderness seems to peek through, and my icy façade begins to melt.

"Look, I know you're upset, but it's the way it is. You have to accept it and find a way to work around it. And I'll help you do that."

The softer tone he takes works wonders. I'm actually willing to listen now.

"What are you planning to do?" I ask.

"I'll come over to your apartment and help you every day. I can run stuff to the post office, clean up your place, type emails for you, do social media posts."

"So you'll be like my personal assistant then?"

He crosses his arms, his face still stern. "If that's how you want to think of it, sure."

"I don't think that's going to work for me."

"Shay, be reasonable."

"We're exes, Wes. We haven't spoken a word to each other in more than six months and now you're going to be my home health aide?"

"Do you have a better idea of how to cope while you recover?"

I sigh my defeat. I can't manage this alone. And if he's offering to help me, I'd be a fool not to accept.

"We need to set some ground rules first," I say.

He leans back in the chair, eyes still on me. "Like what?"

"We have kind of a complicated history. There have to be boundaries."

"Fine. I'll call or text before I come over."

"You can't carry me all the time."

"Why not?"

I contemplate telling him how flustered I get every time he touches me, but I hold my tongue. That would definitely be crossing boundaries. I need to move on, not dwell on what I miss about him, about us.

"The less we touch each other, the better," I say.

The clench of his jaw and the way his eyes dart away for a second tell me he doesn't agree, but I don't care. I need to protect myself if there's any hope of this arrangement working out.

"Fine," he says.

"No staying at my place overnight. No relationship talk at all. I don't want to dwell on the past, okay?"

The expression that passes over Wes's face looks a lot like uncertainty, but he frowns it away before I can be totally sure.

"Do you have any rules you want to add?" I ask.

"Just one. If you fall or hurt yourself, I'm picking you up."

I roll my eyes, but nod anyway.

A nurse pops in to hand me a pamphlet on how to care for my injuries, then gives me a crutch.

Wes swipes the pamphlet from my hand, and I prop myself up on the crutches. He gestures forward. "Lead the way."

~

SEVEN DAYS of Wes as my personal assistant and it's only marginally weird now. We haven't broken any of our rules. Every day he stops by to help me with emails and chores around the apartment before taking the packages I've prepped to the post office. Every day we engage in polite, brief conversation.

He even came up with a cute idea of posting a photo of me sitting at my workspace, my arm and leg wrapped, then posting it on my social media to explain the delay in my work. He was right —everyone understood. I received an outpouring of support. Not a single client of mine was upset.

If we didn't have our history, this would all feel almost professional.

This morning I texted him to bring an extra-large duffle bag to transport the packages. Wes stares at the stack of sealed envelopes and boxes sitting next to my desk, eyes bulging. "So just a few extra today, then?"

From my desk, I roll my eyes, failing to stop the smile that rips loose. "Very funny. I'm trying to be as productive as possible."

"I can see that."

He crouches down and starts to shove the envelopes in the duffle bag. He shoots a soft smile at me. "You've got a lot to be proud of. What's you're doing is impressive."

I could swear my heart beats faster at the sound of his words. A hot flush makes its way up my chest to my cheeks. I turn away to my desk, pretending to rifle through a random stack of papers.

"That's nice of you to say. Thanks."

When I look up at him, he's still standing there, only this time staring. But it's a different kind of stare than the usual broody one he's been employing lately. I remember this one well. Tender and kind with unspoken amounts of affection resting behind those rich brown eyes.

I should look away—but I can't. Because despite the rules I set, despite our boundaries, I want him to look at me like this, like I'm the only thing in a million-mile radius that he cares to lay eyes on.

"I'm not being nice, Shay. It's the truth. I'm so proud of you, of the artist you've become. You have so much talent and drive. I just wish that—"

His phone ringing interrupts him. I want to yell for him to forget his phone and tell me right now what exactly he wishes.

But he swipes it from his pocket and frowns at the screen before I can utter a word.

"Sorry, one sec," He says, answering the call. "What's up, Colin?"

I pretend to sort through the papers on my desk until he's off the phone, hoping he'll pick up where he left off when his phone rang.

"Sorry about that," Wes mutters.

"No problem." I try to sound as unbothered as possible. I have no idea if I pull it off.

This time I collect all the stray pencils and pens within arm's reach while I wait for him to complete the sentence he started before he was interrupted. But a minute passes and there's only silence. He finishes loading the duffle bag and zips it up. That means he'll be out the door soon. Something inside me aches. I need him to stay. I need him to tell me exactly what he was thinking.

"So...how's Colin doing?"

Such a pathetic transition, but it's all I can think of to get him to stick around longer.

"Pretty good. Business has been picking up for him so he switched me from part-time to full-time."

"Really? That's great."

Since Wes has been back, Colin hired him back on as a project manager for his construction company. I wonder what exactly Wes said to him to crawl back into his good graces after breaking up with me and taking off without warning.

A shy smile tugs at his face as he chuckles. "You sound surprised."

"It's just...I'm glad he hired you back. After you left, I mean."

"It took a little groveling," he says. I wait for Wes to say more, but he doesn't. "It's just nice to be able to pay the bills." He rubs the back of his neck.

Again, there's a silent moment, but this time the tension in the air is painted different. Not the dark shade of strain like before, but something lighter and brighter. Something joyful.

But then Wes blinks, turns his head away to look at his bag on the floor, signaling the moment's over. "I should probably get this to the post office before it closes."

"Right." I let out a flustered chuckle. The moment's passed. "Thanks again for doing that."

He nods, then heads for the door. I spin away to adjust my easel, expecting to hear the hard click of the door. But there's only more silence. I glance up to see Wes giving me that same stare from before.

"What I meant to say earlier was I wish I could have been here with you when you made your dream come true. I'll always regret that. You must have been so happy. And seeing you happy was my favorite thing in the world."

Before I can say anything, he's gone.

CHAPTER SEVENTEEN

"Okay but, like, how did he say it?" Remy asks from the opposite end of the couch, eyebrows wrinkled together in concentration.

I shove a spoonful of Nutella in my mouth, savor it, swallow, and sigh. "Like he meant it."

Remy squints at me from the opposite end of the couch. Yesterday's visit from Wes is doing a number on me. That's why Remy is here on a break from Dandy Lime, helping me decipher just how I should feel about the words Wes left me with before he walked out the door.

I wish I could have been here with you when you made your dream come true. I'll always regret that.

Remy hums before leaning back on the couch. He swipes the jar of Nutella from me and dives in with his own spoon, then hands back the jar. "More importantly, how do *you* feel about it?"

I throw my good arm up in the air. "I have no idea."

"Lie," Remy scoffs. "It's written all over your face. And you wouldn't have texted me this morning asking me to come over to chat about Wes and your conversation if you didn't have an inkling."

I shove his arm. "It's not a lie. I admit, there were some definite, hard-core emotions swirling within me when he said that. I just don't know how to deal with them."

"You both agreed to this weird arrangement you have going on." Remy pats my arm, chuckling. "So is he officially your caretaker? Your personal assistant? No, wait, errand boy! I like the sound of that much better."

He falls back on the couch, clutching his stomach as he cackles. I poke him in the ribs, the one spot I know is his weakness. He yelps and frowns.

"Would you shut up already? It's not a weird arrangement. It was either Wes helping me or I would have been pestering you every day to take on my to-do list."

"Okay, fair point." Remy holds his hands up in surrender. "All I'm saying is that it's clear by his words and your reaction that there's something between you two still."

I deflate at Remy's dead-on assessment.

"It's not necessarily a bad thing," he adds.

"Of course it's a bad thing. I loved him and wanted to start a life with him. Marriage, kids, family, all that. He didn't love me—and he didn't want what I want. Why would I try to make something work with him when we're in two completely different places? Now our best hope is to make it work as friendly exes, but we can't move on to that stage if there are still feelings between us." I frown. "And when did you change your tune? You were nodding your head right along with me before when I said I didn't want to see Wes ever again. You were ready to chuck him out of the bar the night he came in to see me, remember?"

Remy lifts an eyebrow, giving me his trademark doubtful look. But to my surprise, he says nothing.

I screw the lid back on the Nutella and place it on the coffee table. "You're awfully quiet."

Remy sighs. "I admit I had it out for Wes when he came back out of the blue looking for you. I was ready to make him pay for breaking your heart. Even the way he wanted to take care of you after you got hurt had me suspicious. I thought it was a way for him to get rid of the guilt he felt after leaving you."

For a second, he looks away, like he's gathering his thoughts for what he wants to say next.

"When you told me Wes would be dropping by every day to help you, I thought it was a bad idea—at first. But then I stopped and thought about it. Guys do not offer to spend their free time with women they have zero feelings for."

Now it's Remy's words that are throwing me for a loop. He seems to notice because he pats my hand.

"I was mad as hell when I saw him come back and give you that half-assed apology," Remy says. "But there's something behind his actions."

"How do you know that?"

"I don't. It's just a feeling. He went through all this trouble to help you. There's a reason for that. And I think it goes beyond him trying to prove that he's sorry." He pats my knee, then stands up. "Gotta head back to work. Thanks for the Nutella."

"Thanks for the confusing talk."

Remy walks out the door, leaving me alone to think about what he said.

ONE WEEK later and it's clear: there hasn't been anything to read into about Wes's actions. Every day he comes over, we chat pleasantly as we work, and he leaves. He's made zero comments alluding to his feelings about me. Part of me is relieved I don't have to navigate a landmine of emotions with him; part of me is confused as to why he mentioned anything in the first place if he wasn't going to act on it.

I shove aside the thought as I study the sketch I'm working on while lounging on the couch. I squint at the drawing, wringing out my recovering hand. I took a bold step earlier this week and tried to exercise my hand by drawing for a small chunk of time every day. Today is the first day I've done it without the support of an ace bandage and I'm thankful at how dexterous I still am. Still, at least a week to go until I'm back to my normal strength.

Wes finishes up an email while sitting at my desk when his phone buzzes. He glances up at me. "Do you know anything about helicopter fashion?"

I burst out laughing from my spot on the couch. "Um, what?"

Another buzz. Wes's eyes go wide. "Holy shit. Colin is going on a date with Mari Dash. She's taking him on a helicopter ride tomorrow night. He has no idea what to wear. What the…"

My head falls back in a chuckle when I think back to the night I ran into Colin at Mari's concert. After she finished, I introduced the two of them and they hit it off. I give Wes a quick rundown of being invited to Mari's show in Portland and randomly running into Colin. I skip the part where I pathetically asked about him.

"Tell him to wear his white button-up and roll the sleeves up to just below his elbows," I say, recalling how Mari fawned over his muscled forearms later that night. "She went wild for that look the night we met her."

Wes relays my fashion advice to Colin. "Colin has been advised. And that sounds like one hell of a night."

We chat more about how crazy it is that I actually got to hang out with our favorite EDM DJ.

"I should have mentioned it to you before," I say. "It was just… we were in kind of a weird place. What with you coming back out of the blue and us fighting."

"It's cool." Wes clears his throat, his cheeks turning red. He walks over to me and peers at my drawing. "Whoa. That looks amazing."

"It's just a sketch of the living room."

The longer I look at it, the more flaws I see. There's nowhere near the amount of detail I usually devote to even a still life sketch. But I can't push myself. Easing back in little by little is the way to build up my stamina and keep my skill.

Wes sits next to me, grabbing the ace bandage from the arm of the couch. Gently, he grabs my forearm in his hand and begins to wrap it. My skin tingles at his touch, even after all this time.

"So no packages for me to ferry to the post office today?" he says, jolting me out of my thoughts.

"Nope. Only digital files, and I emailed those this morning."

He leans back against the couch, letting out a soft groan when he stretches. "How about a drink then? We made it to the middle of the workweek. We should celebrate."

I chuckle. "You've been out of work mode a long while if you think that making it to Wednesday is worth a celebration."

He bends down to reach the bag he brought. I focus on the black nylon and my breath catches. It's the same bag he packed the day he left me.

I swallow again, letting the sting wash over me. He unzips it, then looks up at me. "What?"

When he looks back at his bag, recognition falls across his face. "Sorry, I…it's the only backpack I have. But I guess you know that."

"It's fine." I nod and blink, forcing a smile.

He walks over to the kitchen, fetches two glasses, and sits next to me. When he pulls out a bottle of tequila from his bag, my eyes go wide.

He must notice my reaction. "What's wrong?"

"It's tequila."

"Is that a problem?"

I shake my head, letting out a flustered huff of breath. I try to smile. "It's just…"

The amber-hued liquid glimmers in the sunlight streaming in through the nearby window. I stare, mesmerized by the honey color.

I clear my throat. "After you left, I said never again. To tequila, that is."

"You did?" He looks so surprised.

"Well, yeah. It kind of became our drink. Remember?"

He nods before his eyes fall to the floor. When they land back on me, a sad smile plays at his lips.

"After I left, tequila was all I drank," he says. "It got to be a problem."

Questions dance at the tip of my tongue. Did he indulge in a week of post-breakup binge drinking like me? Does the mere thought of tequila ever send him into an emotional tailspin? Is he scared that he'll never be able to look at another bottle of that honey-hued devil's booze without picturing my face?

"We're good now, right?" he asks, his expression unsure.

I don't answer him. I just bite my lip and glance between him and the bottle.

"One drink, Shay. Please?" I open my mouth to decline, but he speaks first. "We should be able to do one friendly drink together."

Despite my hesitation, I agree. I want to be able to share a cordial drink with Wes. This is as good a time as any to try.

"So you carry tequila in your bag at all times?" I ask.

"Bad habit."

He pours me a glass first. I'm about to sip when I catch his furrowed brow. I stop before it hits my lips.

"No toast?" he asks.

"What is there to toast?"

He shrugs, his smile taking on a flustered edge. "Just thought the mood called for it."

I raise my glass. "To friendship."

"That's so cliché."

"To exes getting along."

He blinks and I could swear he flinches. "I approve."

We toast and sip. The burn coats my entire mouth, hitting all the way to the back of my throat. I wince through my swallow, it's so potent.

"Damn," I huff.

"It really has been a while for you." Wes laughs, taking another long sip without a hint of hesitation.

"This is like water to you, good lord."

He shrugs.

"Tell me about it."

"About?"

I raise an eyebrow at him. "About your tequila binge after you left."

He sighs, his jaw clenching through his smile. "There's not much to tell. I packed three bottles of tequila along with my bags and bought a bus ticket to southern Utah. I spent my days hiking the national parks and camped out in whatever quiet remote area I could find in the evenings. I'd swig tequila after dinner until I got drowsy and eventually passed out. Mornings weren't fun."

My jaw drops. "You did that every night?"

"Pretty much. Whenever I was close to running out of tequila or supplies, I hitched a ride to the nearest town. Bought another bottle and did it all over again."

"How long did you do that?"

He stretches back, gazing up at the ceiling. "A solid month. I cut myself off after that."

"Hiking with a hangover every morning for thirty days straight sounds like a special form of torture."

"It was. I deserved it though."

"Tell me about your hiking trip," I say, hoping to change the subject to something more pleasant.

A soft smile takes over his face. "It was incredible. Utah is the most gorgeous state I've ever visited."

He talks about how Zion National Park was packed to the brim with tourists, but it was so beautiful, it didn't even bother him.

"Canyonlands is prettier, in my opinion," he says. "And a lot less crowded."

"What about Arches? Did you get a pic standing under the Delicate Arch? I feel like that's a requirement for everyone who visits there."

"Absolutely."

He pulls out his phone and swipes through an endless reel of photos. I gawk at the endless expanses of red rock.

"These are stunning," I say.

"I hiked that area for months and I still feel like I didn't see it all," he says. "I'd kill to go back."

"I'm jealous."

"Don't be. You kicked off one hell of a career in that time."

"True. But I should have gotten out more. It was easy for me to get lost in work. I tend to do that when I'm stressed or trying to distract myself from...well, you know."

We sip our drinks at the same time, letting another silence settle between us. Then Wes turns to me, his stare intense, unblinking, and something more. Something I can't quite put my finger on.

"Shay, I know I did a shitty job of it when I got back, but I still want to apologize. The way I handled things—the way I ended things with you wasn't right."

I lift up my hand to cut him off, but he shakes his head. He leans closer to me. We're still a respectable distance from each other on opposite ends of my couch, but his move to be closer weighs heavy.

"No, I need to say this. I was an asshole."

He pauses to swallow, moving even closer to me. I swallow too, hanging on every word as if it's the last one I'll ever get from him.

"If I could go back, I would do everything differently. You deserved—you *deserve* so much better than what I gave you."

His tone is firm yet soft around the edges, so full of emotion. But I can't handle emotional anymore—not from Wes.

Our faces are only inches apart now. When he breathes, I can almost taste the sting of tequila as it floats out of his mouth.

"There's something I've wanted to ask you," he says. "Can we..."

For a second, he hesitates. I take that as my cue to shut down this conversation before I get hurt again.

I press my hand over his mouth, cutting him off. Because we're friends now. And us as friends means no more emotionally charged conversations that leave me a bundle of uncertainty, aching for any bone that Wes is willing to throw me.

His eyebrows wrinkle together at the sudden presence of my fingers on his lips.

"Don't say anything more," I say.

His mouth moves against my hand and he hums what sounds like gibberish, but I shake my head no.

"I mean it, Wes. Our relationship—our past—it's history. I don't want to rehash it, okay? Let's just focus on being friends now, nothing more."

It stings less than I thought it would to say these words. I take it as a sign that I'm doing the right thing.

Wes stills against my hand, his eyebrows smoothing back to their rightful place along that smooth ridge of forehead. He nods, looking back to our glasses, which now sit empty on my coffee table.

He makes a grunt-noise that sounds a lot like a throat clear. "More?"

"No, thank you."

He twists the cap back on the bottle, then shoves it back in his bag. "I should get going."

"Thank you for helping me today."

"No problem." He zips his bag, stands up, and flashes a forced smile at me. "I'll see you later."

The door shuts. Instead of making myself dinner like I would normally do in the early evening, I stay seated on the couch, staring at the empty glass the faintest hint of gold liquid at the bottom.

I did the right thing. I drew boundaries and obeyed them. I sink deeper into the couch, unable to move. Then why do I feel so hollow?

CHAPTER EIGHTEEN

I set down my paintbrush and stretch my neck from side to side. Another cityscape painting is nearly done and my muscles are in knots as a result. I'm just starting to feel well enough to paint and sketch again, but as much as I love it, it's hard work getting back into it after an injury.

I'm wringing my hands out when there's a knock at the door.

"Come in," I holler, pressing my palms against the tops of my thighs to stretch them.

Wes enters. "Still at it?"

"Always."

There's been no more shared tequila between us since last week, and that's for the best. No more awkward moments. Just polite conversations that prove we're moving on.

I press a fist into the muscle knot that has so conveniently wedged itself where my neck meets my left shoulder.

When I pivot to face him, Wes is frowning.

"You're not pushing yourself too hard, are you?" The concern on his face and in his tone sends a warmth straight to my chest.

"Of course not. This is all part of recovering. Working my wrist and my leg every day so that I don't get stiff. It's going to be sore at first, but that's part of the process. I'm feeling better every day and by next week I'm sure all soreness will disappear."

Wes crosses his arms then starts to put together packages to take to the post office. I continue with my painting.

He turns back to me, his face still painted in concern. I stare back in confusion until I realize I'm absentmindedly rubbing my sore wrist. I stop immediately.

"Have you thought about doing something to ease the stress of your muscles after you work them every day?" he asks. "It would be best for your recovery, I think."

I turn back to the painting. "Like what?"

"Like massaging them."

"I rub my ankle and my wrist after I finish painting or sketching. I'm fine."

The soft sound of Wes's frustrated exhale hits my ears. "No, I mean like you should see a massage therapist. I think that would help a lot."

"Business is going well, but I'm not made of money. I can't pay a massage therapist to rub my wrist and ankle every day."

Another frustrated sigh. "Then how about I do it?"

"Wes, a massage isn't exactly staying within the confines of friendship, especially for exes."

"I'm just trying to help you recover in the safest way possible."

"Do you offer Colin or any of your other friends massages when they're hurt?"

"No. But we've definitely gone above and beyond more times than I care to remember."

"Like how?"

"Let's just say there have been nights of hard drinking where we've had to help each other get cleaned up, undressed, washed up vomit, that sort of thing."

"You mean…"

He sighs. "I've helped Colin and my other friends remove their vomit-soaked clothes and get them into a shower. They've done the same for me."

I laugh. "That definitely counts."

"A wrist and ankle massage doesn't seem so awkward now, does it?" He smiles and shrugs.

"I guess not."

He helps me over to the couch and takes a seat at one end while I sit on the other. I stretch my legs out to his lap. Gently, he pulls my sock off and presses his thumbs against my ankle.

I wince at the pressure, then hum a second later when the muscles release.

His eyes dart to me. "Sorry, did that hurt?"

"No, it actually feels good. Like, a tension release."

A gentle smile stretches across his lips. "Good."

He resumes and the tightness slowly melts away. I hum my satisfaction.

"That good, huh?" He laughs.

"You were right. I definitely needed this."

His touches turn firm, dialing up that hurt-so-good feeling I crave.

I peek up at him through half-lidded eyes. "What do I have to do to make you turn this into a full-on foot massage?"

There's a pause, and his eyes turn serious. "Just ask."

There's an edge of intensity to his expression. It makes my mouth go dry and my heart beat faster.

This is such a couple-y thing to do, sit on the couch and indulge in a foot massage. We should know better. We *do* know better. But it just feels so damn good.

"Please?"

"Please what, Shay?"

His tone matches mine in softness and edge. His hand stills.

"Please can you massage me some more?"

Another moment passes with no words, just our stares connected, his fingers on my skin.

"Of course," he says.

With his thumbs, he applies firm pressure to my instep. I wince through the release, my heart racing as he holds tighter against me.

"Like that?" His eyes are fixed on me, his voice like gravel.

I nod, unable to verbalize. Something in this massage has set fire to our boundaries, to every empty promise we made to be just friends and nothing else. I'm already aching for more.

His fingers slide to the pads of my feet; I bite my lip to keep from moaning.

He catches on. "You don't have to hold it in."

His words, his stare, his presence all hit an invisible release button within me. I let out a breath, then moan. Such powerful, heavenly hands he's got.

Closing my eyes, I lean my head back. I say nothing when he takes my other foot in his hand and begins to rub. This time I don't hold it. My moan is low and soft, my breath shallow.

I want this more than anything. And I think Wes does, too.

Minutes pass, then his hands still. I peel my eyes open.

His stare captures me. "Come here."

I climb on his lap, straddling him. My heart thuds faster by the minute. I shouldn't be doing this. But I don't care. I want to.

His chest heaves up. A pink flush makes it way up his throat, then his cheeks. I lean forward, pressing my lips against his. The contact is so soft; it barely counts as a kiss. But it's exactly what I want. The hint of a kiss, soft enough to ease us back into it after months upon months of zero kisses.

He moves his lips against mine and there's a jolt to my chest. It's so powerful, I grip the arm of the sofa to steady myself. My chest swells and thumps, and then I freeze.

This can only lead to one thing: a reminder that I loved him once and I'm liable to love him again if I let myself get too close to him…like now.

I jerk away from him, planting my hands on his chest. No

matter how many boundaries we invent, no matter hard I try, I'll always want more from Wes. I was a fool to think otherwise.

I scoot all the way on the opposite end of the couch. He turns to me, his face twisted in confusion and worry.

"I'm sorry…did I…did I do something wrong?" he stammers.

I shake my head, crossing my arms. "No, it's not…"

He starts to move toward me, but I stop him with a hand held up. "No."

The struggle to understand plays out in Wes's face and body language. He presses both hands on top of his knees. I can tell he wants to reach for me, to comfort, to soothe. But I can't let him. Not ever again.

A second passes with neither of us speaking.

"Shay, please. Tell me what I did wrong."

"I can't fall for you again, Wes."

"But—"

"I won't work for us. It can't. We don't want the same things, remember?"

He opens his mouth to speak but I stop him.

"If I let myself get close to you again, I'll fall for you." I swallow, steadying my voice. "And when it inevitably ends, it'll destroy me to have to get over you again."

"Shay, can't we—"

"I'd like to be alone," I say, cutting him off.

He stands up and heads for the door. It closes softly behind him.

I stare ahead, too numb to do anything else, until hot tears begin to streak down my cheeks. After a while, I gaze around my apartment, taking in the meaningless shapes around me. Then I halt on something black on the floor near my desk. Wes's backpack.

In his hurry to leave, he must have forgotten it.

I let out a breath and walk to my desk for my phone. I'll text

Remy and ask if he can come get it and give it to Wes so I don't have to see him again.

But then I trip on the strap of the backpack. I clutch the edge of the desk to steady myself, thankful that I landed on my good foot. Glancing down, I see that the bag is half-open and something fell out when I tripped over it.

When I focus on the stray item, I freeze. It's a foot-long strip of bright blue streamer—a decoration from the surprise birthday party I threw Wes.

Then I notice something colorful spilling out of the bag. A palm-sized chunk of papier-mâché. A second later, the image registers in my memory bank: it's a piece of his birthday piñata. He kept it after all this time.

Memories from that day come flooding back. The shock on Wes's face when he saw Dandy Lime decked out in superhero decorations and party favors. The tears of joy glistening in his eyes. The tender words he spoke to me in the shower after the party.

This time when the tears fall, they're not of pain or embarrassment or agony. They're of disbelief. Wes kept these mementos in his hiking backpack that he carried with him every day for the past six months because they meant something to him.

Because *I* meant something to him.

"I, uh, forgot my bag."

I jerk my head up and see Wes standing over me.

CHAPTER NINETEEN

$\mathcal{I}$n my stunned haze, I must not have heard him come back in. When he crouches down next to me, I realize what this scene must look like: me rifling through his belongings.

"I wasn't—it's not what it looks like," I quickly say.

"I know."

"I tripped over it when I was walking over to my desk and it all just spilled out, I swear."

His hand falls on my arm. So soft, so gentle. "Shay. It's okay."

We both stare at the party favors I clutch in my hands.

"Why did you keep all of this?"

Wes settles next to me. I shift from my squatting position to a sitting one. He gazes at me, renewed intensity in his eyes. And something soft, something familiar, something that reminds me of those perfect months when we were together. Something just for me.

"Because they reminded me of you," Wes says. "And how I felt about you."

An invisible rock lodges in my throat, but I swallow around it. "How did you feel about me?"

He pauses to swallow before answering. "I've never cared

about anyone the way I care about you. When you were happy, I was happy. I lived to see you smile. Every day spent with you was the best day ever."

When he stops speaking, his words linger in the air around us.

"You were everything to me, Shay. You still are."

I shake my head, shrugging out of his hold. "Everything isn't love."

"I did love you, Shay. I still do."

My ears ring in the seconds that follow his admission.

"I've never been in love with anyone before in my life. You're the first," he says. "That night when you threw my surprise party, I knew I loved you. I knew you were it for me."

Wes loved me all the way back then? My memory flashes back to the day we broke up. This time when my throat tightens, it brings tears.

"You loved me...but you left."

He offers a sad nod. "After my tequila drinking binge in Utah, I started seeing a counselor online. Sessions with her helped me realize that when I get scared, I run away. It's what I've done my whole life." His eyes glisten. "It's what I did with you. But I'm not scared anymore. I know what I want."

"What do you want?" I finally say

He glances down at the hardwood floor for a moment before connecting his stare with mine once more. "You. I want a life with you—marriage, family, kids, all that—more than anything."

I blink, letting the tears fall down my cheeks. Tears glisten in his eyes too.

"For so long I was freaked out at the thought of meeting some-one's family, of going all-in in a relationship, of trying to make my own family because I didn't have any of that growing up. I couldn't look to my parents for guidance...my mom was gone and my dad was a disaster." His voice trembles, evidence of the emotion that's undoubtedly coursing through him at his confession, just like it is with me. "I left because I didn't know how else to handle it. I'm so sorry I did that. Leaving you was the biggest mistake I ever made."

He inhales, I inhale, and we pause, letting the moment of silence be our collective breather.

"Why didn't you tell me all this when you came back?" I say.

His eyes fall to the floor for a beat before returning to my face. "I tried. But I was so nervous that I gave that terrible apology. You got upset and ran off, then you got hurt. And when I tried again, you cut me off. You said you weren't interested in anything with me anymore."

All our arguments and stilted conversations from the night I fell hit me like a bucket of ice water to the face. This whole time Wes felt the same way about me—he wanted the same things I wanted.

My heart thuds. Everything I've ever wanted him to say has come raining down over me in the past two minutes. I open my mouth to speak, to say the words trembling on the tip of my tongue, but it's too much. I'm in sensory-emotion overload and if I try too much too soon, I may explode.

But after spending so much time skirting around our true feelings, we need to be open and honest with each other.

"This is a lot to take in, Wes."

"I get it." Wes takes my hand in a gentle hold. "What do you need me to do to prove to you that I mean every word?"

I open my mouth, but the words aren't there. Because I can't think of a single worthy objection. Yes, Wes hurt me, but he came back and apologized. He's nursed me back to health, showing me just how much I mean to him. And he went through counseling to work out his issues—the issues that led to our breakup. He's showing me that he's changed and wants a future with me.

I want that too.

"Tell me," he says. "I'll do anything."

"You don't need to." I reach for his face and turn him back to me. "I love you, Wes."

Wes's brow jumps at my confession. He cups my cheeks even tighter. "You still love me?"

"I never really stopped."

I grip my hands around his wrists. Our stares connect in an unbreakable invisible line. I never, ever want to look away.

"I want you, Shay. Forever. If you can forgive me."

My heart thuds, the pressure like a giant drum beating from within. Again, I'm in tears, but now it's joy powering them, not uncertainty. And it's the single greatest feeling in the entire world.

"I forgive you," I say.

"So you're...you're mine again?"

"As long as you promise to be open with me like you were just now. You promise to work through any issues we have—you promise you'll never walk out on me again?"

"Never, ever."

"Then you're all mine, Wes Paulsen. I want a life with you, too. Marriage, kids, family, the works."

Wes's face splits into the biggest grin I've ever seen him make. His eyes glisten with his own tears of joy. And then he pulls my mouth to his.

The contact between us this time is different from the soft and tentative kiss from minutes ago. That kiss was hesitant, shy, earthly. This kiss, with our lips and tongues moving together in heated unison, is every planet in our solar system. It's the Milky Way galaxy mixed with every star that ever existed.

It's the transcendent joy of having him back when I never thought it would be possible. It's beyond every happiness in this known world. It is positively sublime.

Our hands follow the filthy rhythm set by our mouths. We're grabbing and caressing at each other. We waste no time getting reacquainted with our bodies, even though it's been months upon months since we've touched each other this way. We've already said everything we need to say. Now it's time to let our bodies speak.

For just a second, Wes breaks our kiss. With his hands still cupping my face, he smiles softly. "Can we move this to your bed?"

Biting my lip, I nod. He stands and helps me up, and we take the three steps to my bed. I start to slip off my top, but he softy grabs my hands, stilling me. Again his rich brown eyes pin me. My chest tightens. I never thought he'd look at me this way again, with equal amounts of lust and adoration in his eyes. It's almost too much. I swallow, breathe, and smile.

"I missed you so damn much, Shay."

"You have no idea how much I missed you." I press a gentle kiss to his lips.

He traces his fingers along the hem of my shirt. "Let me?"

The slow way he lips my top off, it's as if he's savoring the action. His gaze scans over every bare inch of my torso. Then he wraps his arms around my waist, pulling me snug against him.

He tugs off his shirt before I can even grab at the fabric. I run my palms up his chest. My mouth waters at the hard feeling, the way his chest hair tickles my skin.

My eyes struggle to take in every line, every muscle, every freckle I missed seeing over these past nine months.

Wes softly grips my wrists in his hands, then leads me to a sitting position on the edge of the bed. My breath catches when I remember him pulling the same move our first night together.

Kneeling down, he pulls my yoga pants off, leaving me in nothing but cotton panties. The slightest dip hits my stomach. I glance down.

"What is it?" Wes asks as if reading my mind.

"I just…I never thought this would happen. I'm still in shock."

He nods, a wistful look playing at the edges of his eyes. But then he unzips his pants and lets them fall to the floor.

"Good shock?"

I reach for the waistband of his boxer briefs, fixating on the generous bulge I remember so well. "The best kind of shock."

He moves above me, pressing me into the mattress, and kisses his way down the side of my neck to my breast. He spends minutes showing just how much he missed me and my body. His tongue and lips work me over, leaving me breathless. He hasn't lost one iota of his touch. Just his mouth on my breasts leaves me cross-eyed and desperate for oxygen. I'm tugging at his hair, begging and moaning for more. And when he kisses down my stomach to my hips, my sounds take on a crazed quality.

When he settles between my legs, I hold my breath. His tongue hits me in the spot I need him most, and I gasp, taking all the air in the room with me. It's greedy, but I can't help it. Every hot swirl and lap is a whole new dimension of heavenly. It's even better than I remembered. I grip the sheets with both fists as the heat warms me from my throbbing clit up my pelvis to my chest.

This shouldn't throw me off so much. Wes was consistently spectacular at this. But after months without him, I almost forgot how good he was, how he could make my entire body quake with pleasure.

Every swirl, every lick, every taste is a reminder. He was always this good. And he always loved me.

Heat turns to flames, and I know I'm close. Wes's fingers dig into my thighs. He hums, seeming to approve of my crazed antics. Pressure builds, the aching intensifies, and I grind harder against his mouth. My hand dives into his hair, and I pull. The growl he lets out is positively carnal. And then I break.

The explosion is fire. I'm flailing and shouting, my back in an impossible arch, hanging onto both the bed and Wes's hair. He holds me steady with both hands around my thighs, letting me ride out my climax—just like he always did. Because he remembers me and my body, the way it moves, the way it thrashes. He never forgot.

The pleasure pulses through me, the waves weakening as the seconds pass. My chest heaves and my back falls against the bed.

He climbs on top of me, and I barely have the strength to wrap my arms around him.

I glance up at him, my vision still hazy. "Fuck, I missed that," I babble.

He lets out a low chuckle, then plants a soft kiss on me. "No way you missed it more than me."

I reach down between us, feeling his steely hardness. When I glance back up at him, his eyes are shy.

"Shay, I'm so sorry, but I don't have any, um, condoms."

I frown at him.

"I just didn't…" He clears his throat. "I never thought to…"

Leaning away, I roll to the side of the bed where my nightstand is, throw open the drawer, then pull out a condom.

"Good thing I'm always prepared."

A second later, I'm back under him. He rips the condom wrapper with his teeth, rolls it on, and lines himself up with me.

And then his eyes meet mine. "I love you, Shay."

He slides in before I can tell him that I love him too. Instead, all I can do is moan and howl at the instant pleasure. He starts slow, each thrust deliberate and firm and smooth. The sensations are almost too much, and I claw at his back and shoulders. There was always emotion behind our sex before, but this time there's love. An all-encompassing love that's mutual. It makes everything that much grittier, that much more vivid, that much more intense.

Every thrust is a reminder of just how far we've come, just how much Wes loves me.

"I love you too," I say between pants.

My words seem to spur him on. As his eyes glaze over, the corner of his mouth twitches up into a smirk. He picks up speed, and the pleasure becomes almost too much. I reach down to rub myself as he leans up and repositions both of my ankles on his shoulders.

"Fuck, Shay. Yes. Just like that."

I try to keep my eyes on him as long as I can, but at this angle, the pleasure borders on mind-numbing. My eyes roll to the back of my head and I swirl my hand until it hits the peak. Once more, I come undone.

This time when I flail, Wes has me by both legs, holding me steady. As the pleasure pulses through me, he holds his pace. Through my haze of ecstasy, I feel his body tense against mine. A beat later, there's a growl and a shudder. And then we both still, our panting the only sound in this space.

Seconds pass before I'm able to see clearly again. But when our stares connect, it's a whole new world. Because as Wes gazes down on me, it's pure affection, pure love for me.

My legs still tremble from the orgasm aftershocks. Wes grips both of my ankles with gentle hands and sets me back on the bed. He lowers himself down next to me and hugs my body against his. I look up and catch him smiling at me. I suspect the smile on my face is just as pleasure-drunk as his.

"I love you, Shay. More than anything," he whispers, his mouth pressed against my hair.

Emotion clogs my throat. "That means…" I drift off before I break.

He kisses my forehead, and I have to close my eyes. It's such a tender action. I never thought I'd get to experience it with him ever again. Even now, even after we've declared our love to each other with our mouths and bodies, it still feels like a dream. And I never want to wake up.

"It's okay," he whispers. "I'm here. Always."

The pressure in my chest eases. "I love you, Wes. You're my everything."

I kiss his chest as he hugs me tighter. Together we doze for what feels like the rest of the afternoon and into the evening. When I open my eyes and sit up to look out the window, it's well into the night.

"Wow," I mumble, rubbing my eyes.

Wes yawns, before pulling me back down to lie on top of him.

I chuckle and glance up at the clock. "It's almost midnight. I can't believe we slept that long."

"I can. We had a hell of a time in bed. That takes a lot out of a guy."

I nudge him in the stomach with my elbow. "So you're not annoyed we wasted the evening?"

With his thumb, he lifts my chin to look at him. "No time is ever a waste if it's spent with you."

I press a kiss to his lips, then nuzzle his neck. When I cough, Wes hops out of bed to fetch me a glass of water. I drain it instantly. He refills it and crawls back in, cuddling me once more.

"You know what would be perfect?" I gaze up at him.

"What?"

"Tequila."

"Believe it or not, I'm out."

I kiss his bare bicep. He lets out a low moan.

"Trust me, if I had known how this day was going to unfold, I would have packed a brand-new bottle," he says.

I lean over Wes to reach my phone from my nightstand. "No worries. Remy's always got full bottles at the bar. I'll text him to drop one off after his shift tonight."

When I put my phone back, Wes hugs my back against his chest. "I can always run to the store."

I turn around to face him, softly clawing at his chest with both hands. "No way. You're not leaving this bed for the rest of this evening."

"Just what have you got planned for your boyfriend, Shay?" He smirks down at me.

Boyfriend. I beam up at him. My face hot, I can't help the joy circling within me. Wes is my boyfriend again.

I plant another long and teasing kiss on him before trailing my mouth down his chest. "You'll see."

CHAPTER TWENTY

From above the rim of my glass, I stare at Wes. Naked in bed, sheets tangled around us, is my new favorite way to enjoy tequila. I clink my glass against his.

"To new beginnings," he says.

I raise a brow. "So cliché."

He laughs, then we take a sip. "It's the best I can do after the number you did on me."

My mind drifts back to our night together. We barely racked up any sleep. Mostly naps between mind-blowing sex sessions.

He drains his glass, sets it on the nightstand, then wraps his arm around me, cuddling me into his chest. He squints at the bottle of Dulce Vida tequila that Remy dropped at my door after his shift. "Damn, that's good."

"You can thank Remy later," I say.

Wes lifts his brow at me. "How do you think he's going to take the news that we're back together?"

"He'll be shocked, I'm sure."

"And probably a little pissed."

I laugh. "Okay, maybe a little pissed, but if I'm happy, he'll be happy. Eventually."

"Are you saying I have some groveling to do?"

"Maybe."

He stares out the window for a few seconds, like he's thinking about something else entirely. "Want to grab some breakfast? Maybe at the diner where we had our first date?"

My stomach growls at the mention of food. It's been more than twelve hours since I've eaten. "Yes, please."

We get dressed and bundle up in our coats. We walk with my sore arm looped in his while I brace myself with a crutch using my good arm. I've hit the four-week recovery mark and could probably do without it, but since there's snow and ice out, I want to be safe. I close my eyes and hum to myself. Us side by side, in step, together. Joy. Contentment. Utter perfection.

Wes stops at the front of a small brick building next to Dandy Lime. "I need to make a pit stop first," he says.

"The bar doesn't open until noon, and Remy won't be up for another couple of hours, so you can't grovel just yet," I say.

He smiles. "Noted. I want to check on something else."

He leads me around to the back alley where there's a back entrance to the tiny building next to Dandy Lime. It's completely empty. Remy told me once what business used to be there, but it was before he bought the bar, and I can't remember.

I follow Wes as he strolls slowly inside the space. There's nothing notable about it. Dingy wooden floors that are begging for a polish, high ceilings, exposed brick walls. It boasts the same unfinished industrial look Dandy Lime did before Remy remodeled it.

Wes heads for the corner of the open space, steps to the side, and then I see it. Two framed drawings leaning up against the wall nearest me. Both don Wes's exquisite face, one in black and white, the other in watercolor.

My breath lodges in my throat. It takes a second, but I get my voice back.

"Wes, what...what is this?"

It doesn't matter how long I stare at the framed artwork—*my* artwork. The artwork I so lovingly crafted and then so bitterly sold months ago.

He takes a step toward the pieces, a shy smile on his face. "I wanted to surprise you."

Inside my chest, my heart is swelling and swelling. All this time I thought I sold those paintings to some random person.

"You're the one who bought them?"

"Yes." His eyes fall to the floor as he rubs the back of his neck.

"But how? You were practically off the grid when you were hiking and camping."

"Every time I'd stay in a town with decent internet, I'd check out your website. It was my cowardly way of staying connected to you when I thought I ruined everything."

I squint at my artwork sitting in front of me. I recall the afternoon I stumbled upon these sketches in my desk drawer. My heart swells. I'm so thankful that even in my post-breakup stupor, I didn't rip them to shreds like I initially wanted to.

"But you didn't have an address the whole time you were gone. How did you even manage to get them delivered to you?"

"Colin's cousin lives in Salt Lake City, so I sent them to his place and he held on to them for me until I could make it over there." Wes clears his throat. "When I saw them, I knew I needed to move fast. Someone would have bought them if I didn't snatch them up first."

He turns back to the wall where my paintings rest. Together we stand, silently staring. I scoop his hand in mine, and he twists his head to me. Uncertainty is the undercurrent of his smile.

"You framed them beautifully." I smile at him.

"It was kind of weird trying to explain to Colin's cousin why I wanted to buy two portraits of my own face. He must have thought I was an ego-maniac."

I squeeze his hand. "I'm so glad you did. I should have never given them away in the first place. I was just…"

Wes squeezes my hand softly in return, and I know I don't have to explain. He understands perfectly.

I rest my head on his shoulder. "So did you have to sweet-talk the owner of this building to hide them up here this whole time you've been back?"

"Something like that." This time he smiles like he's hiding a secret.

He turns so he's standing in front of me. "I thought they'd look great as the first pieces you display in your new art studio and gallery."

"I don't have an art studio or a gallery."

"You do now."

Even as he gestures around the empty space around us, it takes me a second to comprehend what he means. Then I feel the impact like an invisible anvil to the head. It knocks every last molecule of air out of me.

"Wait, you mean…this place?"

His smile widens. "It's yours."

"But how did you—what did you…"

"This is your new workspace, Shay. And your own gallery, too, if you ever want to display your work."

I'm beaming so wide, my mouth throbs. But then logic hits and I lose my grin to a frown. "No, I can't…I can't accept this."

"Why not?"

"Because I can't afford this, Wes. I don't have the money for a studio-art gallery combination space."

A laundry list of real-life problems fills my brain. There's rent for the space, then the cost of electricity and utilities. Then the cost of furnishing it.

"I mean, I've been making a profit from my artwork these past six months, but it's nowhere near enough to justify an entirely separate workspace," I babble. "And I don't think I have enough in savings to cover the rent, the bills, what it will take to get this place up and running—"

Wes shakes his head, cutting me off. "You don't have to worry about any of that."

"What do you mean?"

"I had some savings from all my jobs over the years and I used some of it to buy this place."

My eyes bulge. "Wes, that's tens of thousands of dollars. Why in the world would you do that? What if there's an emergency or you have to pay for an unexpected expense?"

His smile is soft, easy, unbothered. It's like I'm pestering him about something minor, like forgetting to turn off the lights before leaving the apartment.

"Shay, it's really okay. There's nothing to worry about. Colin's company bought this building earlier this year. He sold this space to me for a bargain. There's no rent to pay. And I'm going to fix everything up and help you set it up exactly the way you want. You won't have to worry about a thing."

His explanation makes sense, but still, my head is spinning.

"That means you've been working on this surprise for months," I say.

"That's true."

"Which means you were planning this even before we were back together."

A hint of shyness flashes across his face. "I messed up big time. I wanted to do something to show you how serious I was about making this work with you a second time."

The fog of confusion slowly dissipates, giving way to clarity. "You did all this for me."

Even when I say it, doubt lingers in my tone. Because it's just so beyond belief that someone would take such a gigantic risk for the person they love when they're not even together. Wes seems to sense it because he pulls me against him. His face hovers in front of mine, our lips barely an inch apart. The beat of his heart thuds softly against my chest, amplifying the intimacy of this moment.

"Everything I've done these past few months was for you. I want to support your dreams and goals. I want to see you succeed. I want to be there holding your hand when you host your first gallery opening."

His words hum against my ears. If I weren't holding his body, feeling his breath on my skin, gazing into his rich brown eyes, it would sound too good to be true. But it is true. And it is so, so good.

I yank him by the collar of his jacket and pull him to me. "Okay. But we do this together. Everything is fifty-fifty. Every remodeling project we work on, I help you. I know you've got construction experience and I don't, but as long as you tell me what to do, I can help. And if I do decide to do a showing of my artwork—"

"Not if," he corrects. "When."

I kiss the tip of his nose. *"When* I decide to do a showing of my artwork, we split the earnings."

His thick eyebrows wrinkle together. "No way. That's your artwork that you created. You keep anything you get from that."

I start to object, but he stops me. "I earn enough with my job at Colin's company."

"Fine. But if I do any more paintings or sketches of you, we're splitting the profits."

He chuckles. "Deal."

I turn back to the framed paintings. "Except for those. They're not for sale."

He pulls me into a hug once more. "Deal on that too."

I lean back to look up at him. "This space is just as much yours as it is mine, Wes. I don't want it unless you're a part of it too."

He beams down at me. "I'd love that."

Tightening my arms around him, I cuddle my face to his chest. He rests his head on top of mine.

I glance at the empty space in front of me. "We're moving

pretty fast, don't you think? Boyfriend and girlfriend as of last night, and then business partners as of two minutes ago?"

Above me, there's a low chuckle. "We move fast for sure. But we've got months to make up for and a gallery to get showroom-ready. Tell me how I can make this the space of your dreams."

"It already is." I lean back and gaze up at him. "Because you're here."

He beams down at me before leading me in another kiss that leaves me panting. I pull away from him to stroll around the space and walk around, taking it all in.

I stop in the center of the room, turn back to him, and promptly fail to reign in the wicked grin on my face. "I have a lot of ideas for this building, actually."

I shrug off my jacket and unbutton my blouse. Wes's eyes bulge, then the naughtiest smirk spreads across his face.

"But we should christen the space as ours first. Don't you think?"

EPILOGUE

4 MONTHS LATER

"You did it, cuz!" Remy pulls me into a hug, then holds me by the shoulders while beaming at me. "I'm so, so proud of you!"

He squeezes me tighter and I can't help but smile, even though I can barely breathe.

"Thank you," I say before scanning the room, which is bustling with friends, relatives, and prospective buyers.

It's my first art show in the gallery, and I couldn't be happier. After Wes and I christened the space, we must have been on some new-found post-orgasm high and because we set the opening date for just four months later. That gave us barely enough time to tackle everything: finishing the floors, adding track lighting to the ceiling, and painting the walls the perfect neutral shade.

Every time I gaze around the room, I lose my breath. Twenty-five framed paintings and sketches adorn this space. And every time I blink, I can barely believe it. We actually pulled it off.

Thanks to a killer social media campaign, it's not just family and friends at my opening. There are dozens of strange faces making the rounds in the room, staring at my artwork. It's only been an hour into the showing and already I've sold a dozen pieces. I check my watch. Just over two hours left. I smile to myself. I think I have a damn good chance of selling out.

Colin strolls over clad in a suit. "Good news, Shay. That guy with the gray beard just bought your last watercolor cityscape."

I high-five him. "Would you mind putting one of those red dot stickers over the price tag to show that it's sold?"

He flashes a thumbs-up before walking to the painting. Not only has Colin been chatting up my artwork to anyone within earshot this evening, but he also saved us by doing all of the track light installations for free.

He makes his way back over before checking the time on his phone for the millionth time this evening.

"She's running late?" I ask.

Colin frowns. "As usual."

I pat his shoulder. "Her schedule is nuts. She'll be here though, I promise."

Colin nods.

It's been a handful of months since Colin and Mari started dating, and I couldn't be happier for them. One issue they've been struggling with, though, is making time to see each other. Mari's schedule is impossibly busy as she's constantly traveling and performing. But the fact that she bought a house on the outskirts of Bend is a sign that she's taking her relationship with Colin seriously.

Remy points his drink at Colin. "You're dating a jet-setting celeb, man. You knew the drill when you signed up for it."

I frown at Remy, hoping he heeds my silent warning to shut it.

"I'm well aware, Remy," Colin says.

I give Colin's forearm a gentle squeeze that I hope is comforting. I'm about to say more words of comfort, but just then out of the corner of my eye, I catch Mari trotting into the gallery clad in a chic camel-colored trench and silver stilettos. She waves at me before scurrying to Colin.

He turns around and the widest grin I've ever seen him make

appears on his face. They embrace, then kiss. Even in four-inch heels, Colin still has a few inches on her. With his arms around her, his broad frame easily envelopes her.

She slides her hands up his chest and rests them behind his neck. For a few seconds, all they do is stare at each other. Then Mari twists her gaze to me. "Shay, congrats."

"Thank you. It means everything that you would come to this."

"I wouldn't miss it for the world."

She grabs Colin by the hand. "Show me what paintings are still left unsold. I need some new art for the house."

Still grinning, Colin leads her to the far end of the gallery.

"A hundred bucks says you sell out tonight, cuz." Remy nudges me playfully with his elbow. "So, how does it feel? You're a successful artist with a celebrity fan base. I don't know if I'm cool enough to hang out with you anymore."

"I will never be able to out-cool you, Remy. And don't talk me up so much. Mari is one person. And this is my first show. I don't want to jinx anything. Thanks again for supplying the alcohol tonight. People are much more likely to drop a few hundred dollars on artwork when they've had a few."

"More than happy to help." Remy hands me a glass of water and I take a long sip. He lifts an eyebrow at me. "If only that were champagne, right?"

I cradle my stomach. Under my sleeveless red cocktail dress, my bump is barely visible. But I see it every time I glance down. And every time, my heart swells.

I beam at Remy. "Best reason to give up champagne, in my opinion."

"You know I'm kidding." He pulls me into a side hug. "I couldn't be happier for you. So many exciting things happening in your life. Your career is taking off, you moved into a new apartment with Wes, and now you've got a bun in the oven. Your life is a dream come true."

My eyes water at his words. I never thought I could be so happy.

From across the room, I spot Wes. He's talking to my cousin, who's holding his toddler daughter. Wes high-fives her, and she giggles. He can always make her laugh, even when she's fussy. Warmth courses through me at the sight. He's going to be an amazing dad.

When he looks up and spots me, he winks, then heads straight for me.

"Once you give birth, your first drink is on me." Remy indulges in a long sip from his drink.

"And Wes's, too. Remember how he gave up alcohol during my entire pregnancy so I don't have to go it alone?"

"The way you two go out of your way for each other is sickeningly sweet," Remy says.

Just then Wes trots over and scoops me into a hug. He plants a perfectly sweet, perfectly PG kiss on me. Suitable for all the family we're surrounded by tonight, even though I'm aching to jump his bones. The cut of his charcoal gray suit is lethal on his lean and muscled frame. I grip on to his shoulders to keep my hands from wandering to the naughty places they'd rather explore.

"Careful. There are kids around," Remy jokes.

"They'll live," Wes says, his eyes still on me.

Remy gives him a playful shove before walking away to chat with family. I smile to myself, relieved that it didn't take long for Wes to crawl back into Remy's good graces. Remy was the first person I told about mine and Wes's reconciliation. He was reluctant at first, just like any protective cousin and best friend would be. But then I revealed Wes's romantic gesture of purchasing the empty building next to Dandy Lime for me to turn into my very own studio and gallery space. All was forgiven after that.

Even better because a month and a half after that, we had shocking news to deliver to my family: I was pregnant.

Even now, the memory of seeing the positive pregnancy test

has my stomach in happy knots. When I close my eyes, I can recall perfectly the joy on Wes's face when I showed him. And then he hugged me and kissed me for a solid minute.

"I'm so, so happy, babe. You have no idea," he said between kisses.

He pulls me tight against him, and I run my hands up the lapels of his suit jacket.

His palm settles softly on my bump. "How are you feeling?"

I bite my lip to keep my smile from growing too comically wide. Ever since I got pregnant, he's been so attentive, always asking me how I'm doing, fetching water and snacks for me constantly, and offering daily foot massages. And he insists on coming to every single ob-gyn appointment with me.

I pat his hand, still on my stomach. "Pretty freaking great."

We both do another scan of the room. I catch my mom excitedly whispering to my dad. After finding out I was pregnant, I didn't think my heart could get any bigger. But right now as I watch my family and friends showing their support for me, it's almost too much. I am at maximum capacity, in danger of bursting if even one more sweet thing happens.

Wes gazes at me with concern. "You're not still nauseous, are you?"

I cup my hand against his stubbled cheek. Now that it's July, he's shaved his beard in favor of a five o'clock shadow that's just as dashing.

"I'm good. Luckily my morning sickness has been sticking to the mornings, not all day like some poor moms-to-be."

He wraps his arms around my waist. "Good. Because after this, I'm taking you out to the diner down the block and we're having a pancake eating contest to celebrate my girlfriend's first wildly successful art show."

I moan. "That sounds amazing."

He opens his mouth as if to speak, but then clamps it shut.

"What is it?"

"I don't know if I like the sound of that."

"The sound of what?"

"Girlfriend."

"What are you talking about?"

"Let's ask everyone what they think."

Wes turns around and calls for the attention of everyone in the room. He steps in front me, his bright smile rivaling the brightness of the track lights above us.

"Everyone, thank you for coming to my brilliant and talented girlfriend Shay's first art show. I…" He stalls and frowns before turning back to me. "You know, 'girlfriend' doesn't seem like a good enough word to describe what you mean to me anymore."

He sticks his hand in the inside pocket of his jacket, pulling out a black velvet box. Immediately the tears hit. I have to cup my face with both hands, I'm on the verge of sobbing from pure shock and joy.

Wes drops down to one knee in front of me. The expression on his face is clear now. Hopeful. But he doesn't need to be. He should know by now I'll say yes.

"Shay, you made me the happiest man in the world when you told me you were pregnant. Now I want to make you happy forever. I can't wait to start our family together. Will you marry me?"

I'm nodding before he even gets the words out. Cheers fill the room as he slips a sparkly cushion-cut engagement ring on my finger. He jumps back up to his feet, and pulls me in for a kiss. We stand there hugging for what seems like minutes, a barrage of cheers and congratulations echoing around us.

"How'd I do?" he whispers in my ear.

"You were perfect," I whisper back.

"So you were surprised then?"

"Stunned." I glance down at the ring. "It's gorgeous, Wes. I love it."

He leans back, taking my face in his hands. His eyes glisten with raw emotion. It's enough to make me collapse right here on the floor in front of all these people. But I don't budge because he's got me. He always will.

As long as we stay in this embrace, everyone around us stays away. It's like they know this moment is ours and they don't want to invade just yet.

Wes squeezes me tighter in his arms. "I mean it, Shay. You've made me happier than I ever thought I could be. You're giving me the family I always wanted. It's…it's the best feeling in the world."

The tremble in his voice makes me tear up once more. Because I know without a doubt, he means every word.

"You and our baby, you two are my family. You two are my everything," he says.

I'm dangerously close to another sob. I try for a joke to keep the tears away before I lose it in front of everyone. "So we're even worth skipping out on your favorite tequila for these next six months?"

"Beyond worth it, no question."

I cuddle into him for one last hug before the crowd descends upon us. Nuzzling his neck, I breathe in. "You earned yourself a lifetime of the most expensive stuff after tonight. I don't care if I have to sell a million paintings, you're top-shelf tequila worthy."

He laughs. I close my eyes and soak in his sound, the feel of his body pressed against mine, the joy of this moment, and how it's light years beyond the joy we've shared so far. It's a new bliss, for our future, our baby, our family, our everything.

He leans back, locking eyes with me once more. In his gaze, I feel like his everything. "I'd go a lifetime without it, as long as I have you," he says.

"Exactly how I feel." I pat my stomach once more. "But luckily after the baby comes, we won't have to choose. We can have both."

Wes beams. "Sounds like perfection to me."

DID YOU ENJOY READING THIS?

Then please leave a review on your retailer of choice! And read on for a sneak peek of Sarah's novel *The Boy with the Bookstore*, out now!

ACKNOWLEDGMENTS

Writing this was a labor of love. This is my very first self-published work and I have so many people to thank for helping me make it happen.

First and foremost, thank you to Stefanie Simpson for reading the first draft way back when. It was a mess and I was a mess, but you were so kind and encouraging. You gave me the motivation to continue writing this when I wanted to give up so many times. This is for you.

Thank you to my agent Sarah Younger and your amazing team at NYLA. You and your squad are brilliant and beyond talented. You helped make this novella what it is, I couldn't have done it without you.

Thank you JL Peridot, for being the kind of friend and author I never thought I'd be lucky enough to meet. You are every kind of awesome.

Thank you to all the people who read this novella when it was called *Tequila* and it was a serial on my blog. Your comments gave me so much joy as well as the confidence to turn it into a full-fledged novella.

Thank you to Melody Jeffries for designing this beautiful cover.

To my friends and family, thank you for supporting me, loving me, and being proud of me.

Thanks to Dan + Shay for writing and recording that amazing song "Tequila," which inspired me to write this novella.

And last but not at all least, thank you to everyone who

purchased and read this novella. For so long I've dreamed of self-publishing, and when I finally made the decision to do it, I was so nervous that no one would care or want to read it. Thank you for showing me that you do care and that you still like reading my words. I love you all.

ALSO BY SARAH SMITH

Faker

Simmer Down

On Location

The Close-Up

The Boy with the Bookstore

Titles written under Sarah Skye

Sips & Strokes

Vibes & Feels

Titles written under Sarah Echavarre

Three More Months

PART I
EXCERPT FROM THE BOY
WITH THE BOOKSTORE

1

JOELLE

*W*hen Max Boyson walks into my bakery, I almost drop the tray of croissants I'm holding and try not to pass out.

It's a daily occurrence for me. Because this is what I have to contend with when he strolls in at seven forty-five on the dot: His six-foot-two frame clad in a black leather jacket, worn jeans covering his long, muscular legs. He wears a knit beanie over that mass of light brown hair, and there's a healthy amount of scruff sheeting along a jawline sharp enough to cut diamonds.

He's a cross between a ridiculously handsome Instagram model and a biker.

And that smile. Oh my freaking god, that smile. Always a half smile. Always the right corner of his mouth quirked up like he's hiding a secret that he's dying to tell. Always deliciously wolfish.

But it's not just his looks. It's his whole demeanor. The way he walks into a room, posture straight, gaze focused and unbothered at the same time. He looms large but is also aware of himself. As physically imposing as he is, he's careful not to crowd anyone when he steps into the tiny space of my bakery. He holds the door for people when he walks in and out. And he always moves out of the way when there's a line. It's an easy confidence he possesses—something I've always ached to have.

He is the epitome of everything I find attractive in a man. And that pinnacle of hotness walks into my world every single morning, setting fire to my skin and turning my brain to mush.

I wish I weren't such an utter cliché. But I am.

I am the physical representation of the phrase "mousy shy girl." If you were to search that on Google Images, my photo would be the first to pop up.

I've got it all: wild hair that hits all the way to the middle of my back and hides my face when it's not pulled into a ponytail, thick-rimmed glasses, a penchant for biting my lip and stammering when I'm nervous, and the inability to maintain prolonged eye contact when a handsome guy looks my way.

That's pretty much what I've done every other day when Max walks in here and places his usual order of an *ube* latte—iced in the spring and summer, hot in the fall and winter—and a plain croissant, just before he strolls next door and opens his bookshop, Stacked, which occupies the store space next to mine in this brick building we both lease in the Jade District of Portland, Oregon.

It all happens like some slow-motion scene out of a movie. Max half smiles. I instantly forget that I often have a store full of customers to help. He makes casual conversation, asking me about the morning rush, what new pastries I've got on the menu that day, if the pigeons in the dumpster behind our building have dive-bombed me when I took out the trash. And like the unsophisticated and painfully awkward human that I am, I burn hot all across my cheeks and neck and chest. I giggle, then stammer my way through the conversation all the while trying not to stare unblinkingly at him so I don't come off like a psycho.

And then he leaves, my heart resumes a steady beat, and I will myself to act like a normal human being again.

It's all very embarrassing, the fact that I devolve into a flustered teen every time I'm in his presence.

But not today.

No, no, no. Today marks something new. Today, I'm going to actually do something about my crush on Max Boyson that kicked off ever since he started renting out the space next to me a year and a half ago. I'm going to ask him out.

It's a daunting prospect for sure. We're technically work acquaintances and if he shoots me down, that's going to be awkward as hell. But during our daily chats, I could swear I feel a flirty edge from him. Like, he's pulling back from obviously flirting with me because he doesn't want to come off like a creep who's hitting on the woman who works next door to him. And I definitely appreciate that.

Or maybe he's just being a cordial neighbor.

I deflate the slightest bit, then immediately straighten back up. No. None of that disparaging talk. I've done that enough my whole life. It's time to go against my play-it-safe personality and do something bold for a change.

Setting down the tray of croissants, I grip the edge of the metal countertop and flash a quick smile at Max when he strolls to the end of the line. I'm hyperfocused as I quickly transfer half of the croissants to the nearby display case before helping the next customer, who's a few people ahead of him. As I ring up orders and hand out pastries, I will myself to keep cool.

Breathe in for one, two, three . . . breathe out for four, five, six . . .

Yes, I'm aware of just how pathetic it is that I, a thirty-two-year-old woman, have to coach myself through a calming breathing exercise in preparation to ask a guy out. But it's no surprise given my dating history. I've only ever asked a guy out face-to-face once in my life . . . in high school. Yeah, I've asked men out since then, but it's only been a handful of times via dating app DMs. That's completely different from making direct eye contact with the ruggedly handsome and tatted-up bookstore owner I've been lusting after and saying the words "Hey, you wanna grab a drink sometime?"

Just the thought sends my nerves crackling, like a match falling into a box of fireworks. I swallow back the somersault in my stomach and greet the next customer, quietly counting down as Max inches closer and closer.

And then, finally, he's at the front of the line, just a foot away from me. I look past him and see that no one else is in line. That means I won't have to ask him out in front of an audience. Thank god.

Slowly, silently, I breathe in and take it as a sign that this moment was meant to happen. I muster every ounce of nerve I have and make eye contact with him while smiling.

"Joelle. Hey."

I will my eyes not to flutter. I love it when he says my name in that soft, low tone that's practically a growl.

"Hey, Max. How's your morning going?" If I could, I would high-five myself right now. My voice isn't one bit squeaky, like I assumed it would be. I sound cool and calm, not at all like the nerve-racked nerd that I actually am.

He tilts his head as he looks down at me, almost like he's intrigued. And there it is. That crooked half smile.

"Pretty damn good now that I've got your incredible coffee and pastries to power me through the day."

I bite back a humongous grin as I turn away to quickly prep his *ube* latte—hot, since it's almost the end of May and we haven't yet hit warm temperatures here in Stumptown.

"How's Pumpkin doing?"

I smile to myself at how almost every morning he comes in here he asks about my pet hamster, who I bring with me to work every day.

"She's good. Chilling on my desk right above the space heater, so she's pretty much in heaven."

His low chuckle makes me grin even wider.

I pluck a fresh croissant from the display case, tuck it into a paper wrapper, and slide both over the counter to him.

"How are Muffin and Doughnut?" I ask, trying my hardest not to squeal at the oh-so-cute names he picked out for his rescue pit bull mix and tuxedo cat. I would have never guessed that a guy who looks like a stereotypical bad boy would opt for such sweet pet names. But it's yet another endearing quality that lands in the column of "things that make Max Boyson insanely hot."

He thanks me as he hands over his credit card and I swipe it through the card reader. As he reaches his arm out, I get a glimpse of the black ink that peeks out from his jacket sleeve. It's a hint of that elaborate sleeve tattoo on his right arm, an intriguing mix of cursive script, several clusters of skulls, massive feather wings, and a stack of books.

I blink and recall just how delicious his tattoo looks when he's wearing a T-shirt or a tank top or a button-up shirt with the sleeves rolled up along his forearms . . .

I swallow and focus back on his face as he speaks.

"They're good. Doughnut is still picking on Muffin most days. He's been stealing that new bed I bought her almost every night."

"Aww, really? Poor Muffin."

"It's hilarious to see a fourteen-pound house cat bully a seventy-pound pit bull. It's like neither of them are aware of their sizes."

I glance up at the door, thankful that no customers have walked in yet so that I'd have to stop our conversation and help them. Our chitchat is easy and pleasant, the perfect segue into my big ask. The nerves inside me slowly dissipate and I'm feeling surprisingly light.

Now to wait for the right moment to actually ask him out.

He sips his latte, complimenting the yummy nutty-vanilla flavor of the ube before taking a giant bite of his croissant. His eyes roll to the back of his head as he moans, and I nearly choke. I'm one thousand percent certain that I've never heard a sexier sound in my life.

I whirl back around to the baking tray and start blindly

stacking more croissants into the display case instead of fainting at the mere sound of Max eating.

"Christ, is that good." He frowns at the croissant like he can't believe the taste of it.

I laugh. "You say that almost every morning."

He shrugs and tugs at his beanie. "Best croissant in Portland, hands down. My death row meal would be a pile of these babies, no question."

I burst into giggles, which makes Max laugh between bites.

"That's a bit morbid." I say, wrinkling my nose.

His smile doesn't budge. "It's true. Best way to go out, death by carbs."

I cover my mouth, I'm laughing so hard.

He peers around the front space of my bakery, which holds a half-dozen small tables. All of them are full with customers chowing down on their own carb-laden goodies.

"So tell me." He leans over the counter, the expression on his face taking on a conspiratorial edge. "What's your death row meal?"

I gaze up at him, relishing how he towers over me since he's nearly ten inches taller. The heat from his body skims over me, and I have to look down for a moment.

"Um, well. I haven't given it much thought."

He wags his eyebrow at me before he sips his latte. "Come on. Play with me a bit."

This time that flutter hits straight at the center of my chest. Okay, that is unquestionably a flirty comment. Yay!

When Max first moved in next door and started dropping by and showering me in half smiles and pleasant conversation, I was giddy. But when I saw him acting the same way around my mom, auntie, and *apong*, I felt decidedly less special. Clearly that's just his personality—gotta charm the neighbors. We share a tiny brick building, after all.

But that eyebrow wag he's blessed me with just now combined

with the growled delivery of "play with me a bit" is a game changer. It's the green flag I need to boost the last reserves of my confidence to ask him out.

"This is going to sound weird, but hear me out: a homemade, fresh-from-the-oven baguette with roasted bone marrow."

He frowns like he's unsure of what I've just said, but the look in his eyes remains playful. "Gotta say, I wasn't expecting that."

I shrug, and pull on the strap of my apron. "I'm full of surprises."

That earns me a full-on grin.

"What's bone marrow taste like?" he asks. "I've never had it."

He's leaning even closer now. Our bodies are less than a foot apart and before I answer, I take a second to just soak in the moment. I'm openly, unquestionably flirting with Max Boyson while we talk about food.

Way to go, Joelle! Look at you being an adorable and sexy flirt! Combining your two biggest passions: food and the hot bookstore owner next door! You're seriously doing it!

"It's rich. And smooth. And thick. And fatty, but in a good way. Like butter, but with a deeper, fuller, nuttier flavor."

Max's inky black pupils start to dilate as he gazes down at me, his mouth cracked open, like he's hypnotized and intrigued at once. I cease breathing.

He clears his throat. "Damn . . ."

I nod quickly. "On hot, crusty bread, it is divine. You need to try it."

He nods right back, like he's in a trance. I'm in a trance too. I can't seem to stop looking at him as I wax poetic about one of my favorite food combinations.

"How is it served?" he asks, his voice between a groan and a growl. "The marrow, I mean."

I watch, mesmerized at the slow movement along his stubbled throat.

I swear I can feel my skin tingling as my internal temperature rises. Who knew talking about bone marrow could get me this worked up?

"Sometimes they cut the bone lengthwise and you can just scrape your knife along the hollow part of the bone and out comes the marrow," I say. "And sometimes they cut it into chunks and the marrow's in the middle, so you scrape out as much as you can, but there's almost always some left, so the best way to get it out is to just put the bone in your mouth and suck it out, really get your tongue in the hole and lick and . . ."

I trail off when I realize what I've said.

A few heads pivot in our direction from the nearby tables. They've clearly overheard me. I notice too that Max's brow is at his hairline at what I've said.

"Oh my god." I let out a flustered laugh. "Did I really just say that? 'Put it in your mouth' and 'suck it out' and 'get your tongue in the hole and lick' . . . Wow. I, um, that's not what I meant to . . ."

When Max's eyes go wide, that's when a tidal wave of internal panic unleashes inside me. "I mean, that's absolutely what you *should* do if you eat marrow. Just, like, suck out the marrow and tongue it out—that's what you need to do to get as much off the bone as possible. Sorry, I just made it sound weirdly sexual and awkward talking about sucking and tonguing and licking. I swear, that's absolutely not what I mean to imply . . ."

And now the entire bakery is staring at me. And Max is gawking at me like I've grown another head.

On the inside, I've deflated like a stabbed balloon. That's it. My chance to ask out Max is officially blown to hell. I completely ruined the moment with my unintentional sexual innuendo.

I fight the invisible flames of embarrassment engulfing my cheeks and direct an apologetic smile at the tables.

"Um, our culinary chat got a bit impassioned. Apologies."

People slowly turn away from me. And then I muster the last morsels of my now fleeting dignity to face Max. He remains wide-eyed, his mouth partway open, shock clouding his entire expression.

"So um, yeah. Baguette and bone marrow would be my death row meal," I quickly mumble.

I clear my throat and pray that the floorboards suddenly open up and swallow me whole so I can escape the utter mortification of this moment.

Max nods once, a dazed expression on his face. "Okay . . ."

For a few seconds we say nothing. And then he backs slowly away and forces a polite smile. "Have a good day, then."

With a shaky hand, I wave good-bye, then dart straight through the kitchen doors and crumple to the floor, cradling my face in my hands. And then I groan.

"Real smooth, Joelle," I mutter.

My phone buzzing from the metal table in the middle of the kitchen pulls me out of my humiliation stupor. I lean up, snatch up my phone, and read the text from my best friend, Whitney.

Whitney: So? How'd it go? Did you ask him out??

Me: I almost did. And then I ruined it by talking about oral sex and bone marrow.

Whitney: ???

Me: I'll explain later.

Whitney: Hugs <3

I sigh, grateful for a best friend who for the past twenty years of our friendship has loved me unconditionally despite my near-constant awkwardness.

I force myself back out to the front of the shop, plaster on a fake yet polite smile, and continue with the workday, all too aware that in addition to mousy shy girl, I am officially the world's most cringe-y human being.

ABOUT THE AUTHOR

Sarah Smith is a copywriter-turned-author who wants to make the world a lovelier place, one kissing story at a time. Her love of romance began when she was eight and she discovered her auntie's stash or romance novels. She's been hooked ever since. When she's not writing, you can find her hiking, eating chocolate, and perfecting her *lumpia* recipe. She lives in Bend, Oregon with her husband and adorable cat, Salem.

Connect Online: sarahsmithbooks.com

 twitter.com/authorsarahs
 instagram.com/authorsarahs